MOUNTAIN COUNTDOWN

ALSO BY J.R. PACE

Mont Blanc Rescue Series

Book 1: Mountain Struggle

Book 2: Mountain Impact

Book 3: Mountain Trial

Book 4: Mountain Shadow

Book 5: Mountain Deadpoint

**

Sharp's Cove Series

Book 1: One Night Years Ago

Book 2: Two Favors Repaid

Book 3: Three Times Ablaze

**

Grim Reapers Series

Book 1: Storme's Match

Book 2: Sawyer's Mistake

Book 3: Prado's Choice

**

Standalone Novella

Cold and Bitter Snow

MOUNTAIN COUNTDOWN

MONT BLANC RESCUE NOVELLA

J.R. PACE

Mountain Countdown

Published by J.R. Pace

Copyright 2022 by J.R. Pace

Cover design by Maria Spada

ISBN: 978-84-124955-3-9

Note to readers: This book contains adult scenes and language, and is intended for adult readers.

AUTHOR'S NOTE

Rising 4,809 meters above sea level, Mont Blanc is the highest mountain in the Alps and second highest peak in Europe. Considered by many to be the birthplace of modern mountaineering, it's easily accessible to visitors (over 30,000 people summit every year), but it's not by any means an easy climb, and over 100 people die every year trying to climb it.

In this prequel novella to the Mont Blanc Rescue series, you'll meet the characters from the Chamonix Peloton de Gendarmerie de Haute Montagne—PGHM for short—the search and rescue team that responds to emergencies on Mont Blanc. The PGHM is real, and the men and women who work there, running hundreds of rescue missions every year, are the real-life heroes that inspired my story.

I hope you enjoy the novella, please click here (https://www.jrpace.com/mont-blanc-rescue/) to learn more about the rest of the books in the series, and sign up here (https://www.jrpace.com/) to stay in touch and get up to date information about my new releases.

Happy reading!
JR

Live your life by a compass, not a clock

-- Stephen Covey

1

Sierra

Unable to hold back a disappointed sigh, Sierra Roy closed the last kitchen cabinet.

She looked around the kitchen, wondering if there were any probable hiding places she hadn't thought of.

No. She'd searched the obscenely large house from top to bottom.

Three thousand feet of luxurious mountain living, and not a single bite of chocolate in sight.

She closed the door to the kitchen, glad to leave all that stainless steel behind, and made a mental note to go shopping sometime soon. Rosa, her parents's maid, still came to clean a couple of times a week, but Sierra had been clear she didn't want her to do any shopping or cooking for her.

Sierra sighed. She needed to get out of here. She'd consider herself a fortunate woman if she never saw rustic wood and stainless steel together again.

You're twenty-five years old and still living in your parents's place.

Of course you need to get out.

But, to do that, she first needed to finish her mountain guide certification and get a full-time job.

She walked across the living room to the large floor-to-ceiling windows and stared out at the white valley below. It was a killer view.

This, I will miss.

The rest of the house, with its large vaulted ceilings, imposing fireplaces, flashy art pieces and, most of all, that ridiculous indoor swimming pool hidden under the retractable dance floor in the downstairs lounge area ... Sierra wouldn't miss any of that.

A sudden thought struck her, and she all but ran to the ski room to find her red ski jacket, emblazoned with the ski school logo.

There was a chocolate square in the left pocket.

Found you.

Dark chocolate—her favorite.

Sierra unwrapped it with care and placed the smooth chocolate under her tongue, groaning at the earthy, spicy taste.

She knew she'd been eating a lot of chocolate recently, but told herself she'd been exercising so much, what with her job at the ski school and her training for her mountain guide certification, that she wasn't likely to gain any weight.

Carrying her jacket on her arm, because it was too warm inside to wear it, she walked back out to the living and dining area and sat at the enormous oak table that could seat twelve—not that she'd ever seen twelve people in the house.

She picked up the checklist she'd taken from the same pocket as the chocolate, and flattened it on the table. She knew exactly how many check marks she had and how many she was still missing, but she found it inspiring to look at it, hence why she always carried it around.

First Aid certificate. *Check.*

Navigation certificate. *Check.*

Climbing and skiing were also crossed off. As a holder of the National rock climbing instructor award, she was exempt from having to attend the climbing instruction module. Same with the ski course, by virtue of being a ski instructor.

She'd also completed all the personal development routes and in-person trainings.

You're almost there.

All she had left was the off-piste training, which she wasn't worried about since off-piste skiing was one of her favorite activities, followed by a supervised guiding session with an actual client.

By the end of the week, she could have her mountain guide diploma. She'd leave this house and find her own place.

She looked at her watch.

Shit.

She couldn't be late to class this afternoon—she had three hours booked with a group of ten-year-olds.

She stopped at the mirror in the hallway. Serious-looking dark blue eyes stared back at her as she put on her sunglasses. She'd caught a bit of sun the last couple of days, and was at risk of ending up with racoon eyes if she wasn't careful. A more pressing concern was her long, brown hair, which looked like she hadn't brushed it in a week. Since she didn't have time to find her hairbrush, she ran her fingers through her hair a couple times, then parted it into three equal strands which she gathered into a simple braid.

There.

Better.

Checking one more time to make sure she had everything she needed, Sierra walked outside and locked the door.

Rémy

On a day like today, after spending all day climbing, Rémy Billecart would usually have been on his way to bed, rather than at a bar.

And yet, here you are.

Rémy and his friend, Gael León, had spent the day on the Tacul, an area which boasted the finest collection of ice routes in the range.

Gael was one of Rémy's favorite people to climb with in the world—a professional climber who also happened to be a member of the *Peloton de Gendarmerie de Haute Montagne*, the search and rescue service that responded to emergencies on Mont Blanc and on neighboring peaks.

Though Rémy wasn't part of the PGHM, he was a mountain guide and expert climber, and often got called in to support the team in search and rescue operations. That's how he and Gael had met years earlier, and how they'd ended up becoming friends.

They both loved rock climbing and went out on the wall together as often as their jobs allowed them to, always pushing each other's perception of what was possible.

Tonight, however, his friend's large, infectious smile was absent. Something had been bothering him from the moment their phones first picked up coverage on their way back from the climbing route.

"What is it, Gael?" Rémy asked for the third time, placing a beer in front of his friend. Since he didn't drink, he'd ordered a glass of sparkling water for himself.

Gael's green gaze looked bleak.

"I'm sorry. I think I'm not going to be very good company tonight." Rémy waited patiently for his friend to continue. "I got a message from my sister. My dad had a heart attack this morning. He's stabilized, and they think he'll recover, but it's just so hard not to be there with him."

Shit.

Gael's family lived in Mexico City—a long way from Chamonix, France.

Rémy placed his hand on his friend's arm. "I'm sorry." He didn't add he'd lost his own father to a heart attack years earlier. That wasn't what his friend needed to hear today. "Have you spoken to your mother?"

Rémy knew Gael had a huge family, but that he was particularly close to his mother.

"I called her while you were parking the car. She's pretending not to be worried. You know how mothers are."

Rémy didn't know, actually. His own mother had left him and his father to pursue an acting career when Rémy had been three years old. He'd seen little of her since then, but his father had taken on both roles with gusto until his death three years earlier, when Rémy was twenty-seven.

"What does your sister say?"

"Alicia?" Gael asked, slipping easily into a Spanish accent.

Rémy nodded. He'd met Gael's older sister once,

when she'd come to Chamonix to visit Gael with her husband and a bunch of little kids, and she'd seemed like a straight shooter.

"She says they caught it in time. That people survive this all the time. But that my father's going to have to change his lifestyle after this."

That was good. It meant there was an *after*.

"You've got to believe her, then."

Gael nodded and took a sip of his beer.

"I wanted to get on a plane, but they've all asked me not to come. My dad apparently told them to tell me that it was no big deal."

Rémy laughed. "That does sound a lot like your dad. Take it one hour at a time, Gael. You know you can hop on a plane anytime, should you need to."

"You're right, I know. It's just so hard—" Gael ran a hand through his dark hair, so different from Rémy's own light blond hair. "Listen, I'm not going to be very good company tonight. I think I'm going to go home."

"Let me drive you," Rémy said.

"Thanks, man, but I think I'll go alone. I need some time to think, and the walk will help clear my head."

Rémy nodded, not at all offended. "You know you can call me anytime, right?"

Gael reached over and gave Rémy a hard hug. "Thanks."

"At least take my hat, if you're going to walk home," Rémy said, placing the dark woolen item firmly in his friend's hand. It could get cold in Chamonix in January.

"What are you, my mother now?" Gael grumbled, but took the hat.

Rémy watched his friend leave and sat back down in his seat, picking up his glass. He'd give it a few more minutes, so Gael didn't think he was following him, and then go home himself.

Just as he determined enough time had passed, the door to the bar opened again. Three figures dressed in red walked through the door.

Rémy knew the man and one of the women. They were both long-time ski instructors—of the rare kind, the ones who both knew how to ski and knew how to teach. His eyes moved to the third figure, a younger woman with light brown hair, stuck in a tight braid. Rémy had never seen this woman before. He was sure of this, because he wouldn't have forgotten her if he had.

She wasn't beautiful, per se. He searched in his mind for the right word. It came to him in French, his native language, even though his profession meant he spoke English most often nowadays.

Frappante.

Striking.

Her hair was light brown with flecks of gold. He wondered what it'd look like when she let it loose. She was tall for a woman—slender, even in the bulky ski outfit, but he could see curves as well. And anybody who spent all day skiing had to have serious leg and ass muscles. His gaze moved to the freckles on her nose. They softened her expression, giving her a wholesome, down-to-earth look.

Rémy's mouth dried up. She was like the girl next door, on speed.

She noticed him staring and looked his way. Her eyes were the darkest blue imaginable.

Does that eye color even exist?

He held her stare for an instant—long enough for something electric to pass between them—before forcing himself to look away. He wasn't a stalker, and the last thing he wanted to do was make any woman uncomfortable.

The TV was a good distraction from looking at her. Usually when it was on, it meant there was a football game, except tonight for some reason the news seemed to be on. The camera showed the outside of a fancy chalet. Since the volume was too low to make the words out, Rémy focused on the subtitles, as they repeated that two violent criminals had been apprehended during their most recent robbery. The screen shifted to show the two men being escorted out of the house in handcuffs. Like most other Chamonix residents, Rémy had heard about these men. While burglaries were not rare in the Chamonix Valley, violent robbery at gunpoint was almost unheard of.

On the screen, walking behind the men, Rémy recognized *Commandant* Damien Gray and his lieutenant, Drake Jacobs, from the PGHM. Damien's jaw was clenched tight, his mouth stretched into a grim, thin line. The camera followed both men for an instant before the picture changed for a commercial break.

Rémy resolved to ask Damien and Drake about it the following day. It sounded like there was a story there.

He pretended to watch the commercials for a moment longer, then, unable to help himself, looked back at the woman. Except she wasn't where he'd last seen her. She'd come up to the bar and was standing just a few feet away from him, ordering her drink.

Up close, she was even more stunning.

"Hi," he said, hoping his voice didn't sound as croaky as it felt.

She looked up at him, but she didn't have to look up too far to meet his eyes. He put her height at five-nine to his six-two.

"Hi."

He felt his blood pool south at her husky tone.

"Rémy Billecart," he said, offering his hand.

She shook it easily.

"Sierra."

"Sierra, that's Spanish for mountain range, isn't it?"

She gave him an engaging smile.

"You speak Spanish?"

Rémy shook his head apologetically.

"Unfortunately not. But I climb."

"Ah. My mother's half-Spanish, half-French. She moved to the United States when she met my father."

That explains her American accent.

"And now they live in Chamonix?"

Her expression tightened a bit. "They split their time between Paris and New York." She didn't elaborate further, but popped a couple of salted peanuts into her mouth from the little dish in front of her.

"Would you like one?" she asked, as she caught him staring.

Rémy did his best not to look horrified. She'd just ingested more salt in that single bite than an adult person needed in two days.

"No, thanks. I try to avoid foods with too much salt."

Or sugar. Or alcohol. Or artificial preservatives.

But he wasn't about to add that. Rémy knew he was a bit obsessive about his diet. He liked to think of his body as a well-oiled machine, and didn't want to fill it with junk.

"Oh. Okay," she said easily. This time, when she popped a peanut into her mouth, she shook it gently first in an attempt to get rid of the extra salt. "Peanuts aren't my favorite, anyway. I like other things more. Like chocolate."

As she spoke, she looked him up and down in a way that made it clear she was looking, and that she liked what she saw. Rémy's mouth dried up again as his cock pushed against the front of his jeans.

2

Sierra

This was so unlike her, she felt as if she were standing outside her body, watching it happen to someone else.

And yet, maybe this was exactly what she needed to relax before her big training session tomorrow.

If she were honest with herself, she'd already made up her mind about it before even approaching the bar, when she'd said goodbye to Celine and Ryan, the two instructors she'd come to the bar with. She'd only been working as a ski instructor for a few weeks, so it was nice be included in after-work drinks. She also had the feeling the two of them wouldn't miss her much, once they allowed whatever was between them to develop.

This seemed like a good night to throw caution to the wind. She focused on the man in front of her, making no attempt to conceal the fact that she was interested.

There was something freeing about it. And of course, he was extremely easy on the eyes.

Rémy.

Being tall herself, for a woman, she'd always had something for tall men, and Rémy was tall enough that she had to look up at him. He'd said he was a climber, and he had a climber's body, strong and lean and powerful.

His hair was so blond it was almost white, tied back to keep it out of his face. If he let it loose, she imagined it might fall all the way to his shoulders. Up close, his eyes weren't blue, as she'd first thought—they were literally silver. He had thick, kissable lips and a solid jaw, particularly now that he seemed to be clenching it.

He wants me as much as I want him.

She looked down first at his left, then at his right hand, relaxing when she didn't see a ring or tan line. That was a line she would not cross.

Two consenting adults, out for a night of fun.

And why shouldn't we indulge?

For once in her life, she could have something just because she wanted it, without over-thinking it. He didn't have to know she'd never had a one-night-stand before. Tonight could simply be a moment in time.

She clenched her legs together on the bar stool as the heat built inside her.

"Can I get you another drink?" he asked, his voice low and husky.

She looked down at her almost full beer. If anything, he should offer to get some more peanuts. She'd all but demolished the little dish they'd placed in front of her.

"Do you live close by?" she asked, using a line she'd only heard in movies.

He didn't seem shocked by her forwardness. If anything, his body leaned closer to hers.

"About five minutes away." Those beautiful, strong lips opened in a smile, showing bright white teeth. Her insides clenched again.

"Five minutes is good." She raised her eyebrow to let him know the ball was in his court.

"Would you like to come over and grab a drink?" Not the most original line ever, since they were sitting in a bar, and he looked mildly embarrassed after uttering it, which somehow soothed her. Maybe he didn't do this every night, either.

"I'd like that," she said quickly, not giving herself the chance to second-guess herself.

"My car's right outside."

She picked up her red jacket and followed him, was halfway to the door when she felt the first moment of indecision.

You're going to get into a car with a complete stranger?

This wasn't her, and it wasn't smart, either.

Her steps faltered. Rémy seemed to sense it, somehow, and turned around to face her.

"I was drinking sparkling water," he said quietly.

That's good. That means he's not drunk.

But that's only half of the issue.

He relaxed suddenly, as if he could read her mind.

"Come here," he said, approaching the table where she'd left her colleagues. Ryan and Celine both looked up. Ryan's broad face broke into a smile.

"Rémy! Long time no see. How are things going?"

"Good, good. It's good to see you, Ryan. Celine," Rémy said, nodding his head.

"I saw you out there last week. No idea why you don't take a break from climbing in winter, like most sane people."

"Are you sure you don't want to sit with us?" Ryan asked.

Celine visibly kicked her colleague under the table, but Rémy just laughed, looking completely relaxed. "Thanks, maybe next time. Sierra and I are going to grab a drink at my place," he said.

Sierra inhaled sharply as she realized what Rémy was doing—he'd started this conversation with her colleagues so that she'd feel safe. The tingling inside her intensified.

"Okay, then. See you on Friday, Sierra," Celine said, reminding Sierra that she wasn't scheduled to work for the next couple of days, since she had her training and certification.

This time, Sierra didn't falter as she followed

Rémy out of the bar. When he opened the door to let her through, she went on tiptoes and leaned into his neck.

"Thank you."

"Nothing will happen that you don't want tonight, Sierra. I promise you," he replied in a low voice.

Sierra sensed that she could trust him, and it gave her the courage to walk out the door into the cold.

3

Sierra

"I can offer you some water," he said from the kitchen. "Or ... more water."

His voice sounded distorted, as if he were speaking from inside the fridge.

"Sure, I'll take a glass of water," she said easily. While she waited, she walked around the living space. You could learn a lot about a person by the objects they chose to surround themselves with.

Rémy's flat was small, but neat. Framed prints of mountains grazed most of the walls. The frames were unadorned, designed to take no attention from the amazing images.

"These are beautiful," she said. A sudden thought struck her. "Did you take these yourself?"

"Most of them," he nodded, smiling. He'd taken off his coat, leaving him in jeans and the black T-shirt he'd been wearing in the bar. Somewhere along the line, he'd also taken off his boots and socks. His feet were long, wide, and calloused. It felt suddenly very intimate, seeing them up close.

She looked up, remembering what she'd been about to say. "You didn't take these from a helicopter."

"Not from a helicopter," he confirmed.

Sierra recognized some of the peaks in the images. They were places few humans had ever reached, and this man had climbed them all. Her insides clenched again. She wanted to run her hand across his chest, to touch—

"I like your place," she said to distract herself, not wanting to appear desperate.

And she did. It was as different to her parents's place as the sun from the moon, and perhaps that was what she liked most about it. She hadn't even gone past the living room, but she already knew she wouldn't find any object here that didn't mean something to him. Unlike her parents, who looked at their art collection first and foremost as an investment, and were happy to surround themselves with pieces other people told them were worth having.

She shook herself. This wasn't going to work if she kept thinking about her parents. She straightened her shoulders, determined to focus on the here and now.

"Would you like to go outside?" he asked, pointing

to the small balcony. He was clearly giving her time to sort out her thoughts.

"No." Sierra walked over and placed her hands on his shoulders, as if she was asking him to slow dance. Rémy's hands automatically went down to her waist, as she'd hoped. One of his hands shifted lower to rest on her hip.

His lips connected with the side of her face. He pressed a kiss against her temple, his touch feather-light. Slowly, very slowly, his lips grazed down her cheek, towards the side of her jaw. Sierra held her breath as his lips approached her mouth.

"Can I take this off?" he asked. It took her a second to realize he was talking about the scrunchie holding her hair in place. "I've wanted to do this all evening."

When she nodded, he pulled gently, freeing her hair from the braid.

"God," he groaned, running his fingers through her hair. "Your hair's even more beautiful than I'd imagined. And I have a great imagination."

Sierra smiled, and Rémy chose that moment to lean forward, capturing her smile with his mouth. His lips were strong and firm. He sucked and nibbled gently, until her mouth opened, looking for more. Their tongues met, seeking contact with each other. Sierra moaned. The kiss felt ... it felt like they'd kissed before, in a different life. It felt like coming home.

Her hands tightened on his shoulders. One of her hands skimmed down his biceps, all the way down to his forearm. He had a climber's forearms, strong and thick and veined.

Not surprisingly, she ran out of air before he did and had to step back quickly.

"Where's your bedroom?" she asked, feeling bold.

One of his hands went under her knees and then she was flying. She yelped, then laughed, holding on for dear life as he strode across the living area. Determined to enjoy the ride, she leaned her head against his chest, smelling his manly, spicy smell.

He set her on her feet next to a king-size bed made with military precision. One corner of the duvet was crisply folded back.

"Impressive bed-making skills."

"Just one of my many talents." He reached for her ski jacket. "Here. Let me help you with this. You're not going to need this ... what the hell do you carry in your pockets? Lead?"

She shrugged, bringing out a flashlight, her avalanche beacon, and a small chocolate bar she'd bought on the slopes earlier that day. And that was just one pocket.

"What?" she asked. "I like to be prepared."

If this bothered him, then—

"An avalanche beacon," he said, smiling. "A woman after my own heart." She was impressed he even recognized the little device, but she hadn't come here to chat technology.

"Why don't you see what else I'm carrying?" she

asked, shimmying out of her white turtle neck to stand in front of him in just her sports bra. It wasn't the kind of bra she would have chosen to wear if she'd known she'd end up here with him—instead of showcasing her assets, it rather mashed them together. From the hungry look on Rémy's face, however, it looked like he was enjoying the view anyway.

Under his gaze, her nipples hardened in anticipation. His large hand came to cup her breasts, but the bra was too tight to allow him access. She wanted him to have access. She brought her hands to her back, impatiently seeking the clasp of her sports bra, but he stopped her.

"Allow me," he breathed.

Moments later, her bra joined her turtleneck on the floor. His hand weighed one breast, then the other, making her breasts feel hot and heavy. He leaned down to take her nipple in his mouth, sucking gently, and she felt the pull in her core.

"Rémy ..."

Releasing her nipple, he moved on to the other breast. When her knees started to waver, and she didn't think she could take any more, he released the nipple and started kissing up across her breasts, her collarbone, her neck.

His fingers closed around her erect nipples, pinching them. She moaned in appreciation, then inhaled sharply as he pinched tighter, striding that fine line between pleasure and pain.

He wasn't gentle, but she didn't want gentle. She wanted a man who made her feel.

"Tell me if it's too much," he whispered. His voice tickled her ear.

She whimpered at the mounting pleasure. "More," she begged. Rémy thrust his tongue into her mouth, and she responded in kind. They tasted each other while his fingers continued their assault on her nipples.

Her pussy burned with need. Hell, she needed to come, and she needed it now. She ground her hips against him, looking for the right kind of pressure.

Rémy's hands went to her waist. He unbuttoned her ski pants easily and pulled them down her hips. He didn't seem surprised by the leggings she was wearing underneath.

"You're like a little onion," he said in a low voice.

His words warmed her inside. She wasn't *little*, by any means, but it was nice to be with a man strong enough to lift her in his arms, someone who made her feel small and delicate.

She followed his gaze when he pulled her leggings and her knee-high ski socks down her legs, relieved to find she was wearing a sporty thong. He pulled it down, baring her to him, and she thanked her lucky stars that she'd taken the time to wax a few days earlier. She was smooth all over except for a neatly trimmed patch.

He groaned appreciatively and flexed his hips against her in a primal, instinctive move.

"Your turn. Take this off," she complained, tugging ineffectually at his T-shirt with one hand and his belt buckle with her other hand. He shimmied out of the T-shirt first. She stared, open-mouthed, at the amazing expanse of muscle hiding underneath.

He was ripped, stronger than any man she'd ever been with—wide around the back and shoulders, and more muscled than she would have imagined a professional climber would be.

She put the thought out of her mind as he removed his jeans and boxer shorts in one single move. His cock sprang free, already fully erect. For a moment, she couldn't believe her eyes. He was huge—not just long, but thick as well.

Big all over.

Her pussy dripped, thinking of having that inside her.

"I'm not going to hurt you," he promised, misunderstanding her look. "I would never hurt you."

She kissed him then, more gently than before—just a brief touch to let him know she trusted him.

Rémy pushed her gently onto the bed and lay over her, careful to keep the weight of his upper body off her. His clever hand found her pussy and he brought a single finger inside her.

He paused when it was in to the second knuckle.

"You're so wet and tight," he groaned.

Against her thigh, his cock wept with precum.

"Give me more," she whispered, and he obliged. A second, large digit filled her, went deeper. Then his fingers curled, touching something inside her she didn't think had ever been touched before. It created a delicious pressure that made her moan and arch her hips—it felt at once like too much and not enough.

He pressed his thumb against her mouth and she licked it greedily. An instant later, that same thumb pulsed against her pussy, massaging her clit. Soon, the combination of the deep penetration of his fingers and the rhythmical stroking of her clit brought Sierra over the edge.

She cried out in relief. Her head fell back, her toes curled on the bed and her hands clenched around the duvet cover. And through it all, he held his fingers so still inside her.

"You're so beautiful," he said, kissing the pulse point on her neck.

She smiled, feeling at the same time completely sated but also still hot.

"Come here," she said, wrapping her hand around his thick cock. "I want to feel you inside me."

"Give me a second." He grabbed a condom from his night table and put it on quickly, holding himself much more roughly than she would have done. "Are you ready for me? I don't want to hurt you."

She was so ready she was going to explode. Unable to find the words to express that, she pulled him towards her. "So ready," she whispered.

He'd never wanted any woman as badly as he wanted Sierra right now. She was ready; he was ready—

So why are you hesitating?

But he'd felt how tight she was, and he didn't want to hurt her.

Her arms came around him, bringing him closer to her. He used that momentum to flip them over, so he was on his back and she was on top.

The view, as she sat up to straddle him, was spectacular.

"Let's try it like this," he said, groaning with pleasure as her hands came to rest on his chest. "Take me inside you."

She bit her lower lip with indecision before taking him in her hand and placing the tip of his cock against her entrance.

Rémy clenched his jaw, resisting the urge to drive himself deep into her warmth, wanting her to choose the moment.

While he waited, he contented himself by looking his fill, memorizing details that he knew would fuel his dreams for years to come—the soft waves of her light brown hair as they fell to the top of her breasts, almost but not quite hiding those stiff pink nipples, the slight curve of her belly, the movement of her hips ... and that beautiful pussy, just ready to take him in.

Finally, just when he thought he couldn't take it, that he was going to come before even getting inside her, she began lowering herself ever so slowly onto his cock. Her expression tightened for an instant, and he focused on keeping very still, waiting for her body to adjust, but she didn't stop and soon he was all the way inside her warmth.

Their eyes connected, the position so intimate it was all he could do not to come on the spot.

"You're ... so big," she panted, raising and lowering herself slowly.

Rémy grabbed on to her hips—hard—needing the contact. He let go quickly when she whimpered, but she grabbed his hands and placed one back on her hip, the other one on her beautiful round ass.

He tightened his hold on her and she moaned in pleasure, riding him faster. The sound was like nothing he'd ever heard before.

His hips shifted upwards, driving into her, feeling her inner walls ripple around him.

"I'm going to come," he groaned.

She stilled on top of him, his cock fully inside her.

"Bring me with you," she begged.

Rémy reached between them. His thumb found her clit and strummed it gently. Just as he felt himself reaching the point of no return, Sierra stilled and cried out. Her pussy contracted around his cock, drove him over the edge.

"Sierra!"

He was still coming when her upper body fell on top of him, as if she couldn't hold herself up any longer. Holding her close, he listened to their racing heartbeats.

"That was incredible," she whispered.

"It was," Rémy agreed.

He tightened his hold on her. He'd have to leave her soon enough, but for now, she was in his arms, and he didn't want to let her go.

Eventually, though, he felt himself beginning to shrink inside her, and knew he had to go dispose of the condom. Forcing himself to move, he shifted her slender body off him and lay her gently on her side, dropping a quick kiss to her temple.

"I'll be right back."

When he came back just moments later, she was sitting up in bed. The relaxed expression was gone from her face. Now, she had the look of someone about to run for the door.

"I should go," she began quickly. She sounded almost embarrassed—as if she worried he might be about to kick her out. It made him realize how little they knew of each other.

"Please don't leave. Stay the night."

"The night?" She sounded hesitant.

"I'm not done with you yet," he said.

Anything to make you stay.

He regretted the lie as soon as it was out of his mouth. Though having sex with Sierra again would be no hardship, the real reason he wanted her to stay had nothing to do with sex, and all to do with holding her and getting to know her better.

"I'm going to need a nap first," she said, her lips curling up in a shy smile. He breathed out, relieved—she was staying—and pulled her gently back onto the bed, draping himself around her like a figure of four.

We fit.

After a few seconds, he felt her relax against him. Her breathing evened out, and Rémy was almost sure she'd fallen asleep. Then her voice called out in the dark.

"You're a cuddler," she whispered, her voice laden with sleep.

Thinking nobody had ever accused him of that before, Rémy pondered that statement until he, too, fell asleep.

Minutes later, it seemed, Sierra shook him awake.

"Wake up, Rémy," she said. Her voice was middle-of-the-night husky.

"What?" he mumbled, rubbing his eyes.

"I have to go. I didn't want to leave without saying goodbye."

He was now wide awake. He would have hated to wake up and find her gone. It was a good sign that she'd woken him up—hopefully it meant she wanted to see him again.

"Where are you going?" Rémy had a well-developed internal clock and knew it was still early. A quick glance at his phone confirmed it. "It's five a.m."

She nodded, looking guilty now. "I'm sorry. I have to get home. I have something important this morning."

He realized she was fully dressed, while he was still buck naked under the sheet.

"Let me at least drive you home," he said. His own voice sounded desperate to his own ears.

"Don't get up. I called a cab."

He sat up in bed, careful not to give her too much of a show. "Can I call you? I'd like to see you again."

"Sure," she said vaguely, but made no move to give him her number. "I have something going on the next few days," she began. He must have looked crest-fallen, because she softened her tone. "But I'm sure I'll see you again afterwards."

Rémy nodded. "Sure," he said woodenly. Her rejection stung.

"Thank you for a wonderful night," she said, just before leaving. "I'll close the door after me."

Ouch.

4

S *hit.*

She shouldn't have given in to temptation—shouldn't have stopped to buy more chocolate. Now she was going to be late to her first off-piste training session.

Her mother's words resonated in her mind.

You never get a second chance to make a first impression.

Shut up, Mother.

You're not really here.

It also didn't help that she couldn't stop thinking about Rémy. Her mind was still reeling, her body still tingling in all the right places, from their night together. She'd never been as satisfied, never met a lover who was so strong, and at the same time so considerate.

The whole time they were together, she'd felt his unbreakable control—the way he'd seemed to know, instinctively, just how hard she wanted it, what she needed. She wondered what it would be like to make love to him again, and to feel that control shatter.

Make love?

Are you losing your mind?

If he could hear you, he'd be running for the hills.

And rightfully so.

She looked down at her phone. As of two minutes ago, she was officially late. She'd have to start the session by apologizing to her trainer. Probably not the best way to convince him that she was a responsible adult, fit to become a certified mountain guide.

Willing the cable car to move faster, Sierra broke off a small piece of chocolate and stuck it in her mouth. Sucking on the sweet, spicy square, she willed herself to relax.

It is what it is.

By the time the cable car reached the last ridge, she'd also come to a decision. If the next couple of days went well, and she finally obtained her mountain guide diploma, maybe she would reward herself by calling Rémy and seeing if he still wanted to see her again.

Finally, the cable car entered the hut. She brought her goggles down onto her face, lifted her skis and poles and stepped off the cable car easily, walking fast onto the snow outside.

Now to find her instructor and start apolog—

No.

No.

Please, no.

She wanted to rub her eyes, pinch herself awake, but of course she wasn't about to embarrass herself by doing that, because this was no nightmare—and the man standing right there, a suitably surprised expression on his handsome face, was none other than Rémy Billecart, her one-night stand.

Arghhh.

She wasn't sure if the sound actually came out of her throat or not, but either way, there was little doubt he could read the horror in her expression.

She gripped the skis in her hands tighter. "What are you doing here?"

Rémy didn't reply to her idiotic question.

"You're SJ Roy?" he asked, his voice level.

"Sierra Janine Roy." The words felt like acid on her tongue.

"I didn't catch your last name last night. I didn't realize ..."

"Neither did I," cringing at the sound of her voice. She was aiming for mature and unconcerned, but it came out more like a scared croak. She tried to recall the email the association had sent, couldn't remember if the name of her instructor had been on it. She certainly hadn't paid any attention to it.

Rémy said something else, but Sierra didn't catch it. She was taken back to the time she'd first held up a seashell to her ear, listening for the sounds of the ocean. Except now there was no ocean, and the roaring was in both her ears at the same time.

His voice got louder until she could hear him past her panic.

"Relax, Roy. It's going to be okay."

How is it okay that you had your dick inside me just a few hours ago?

She clenched her teeth to make sure the thought didn't leave her head. She didn't need any more embarrassment.

Focus, Sierra.

So you slept with him.

Big deal.

You're not going to throw away years of work because of a one-night stand.

No matter how amazing it was.

"You're not a climber," she said. Somehow, the fact that he'd lied to her hurt.

Did he lie?

She tried to recall exactly what he'd said.

"I didn't lie to you," he said patiently, as if reading her mind. "I said I climb. I'm also a mountain guide, and a certified instructor."

A mountain guide, and the person responsible for my final off-piste training and assessment.

She wanted to shake herself. "I should have asked.

I should have done a full personal interview. I should have—"

"It's going to be okay."

Out here in the snow, his silver eyes looked lighter than they had last night when he—

She managed to pause the thought just before it became x-rated.

How am I going to get through today?

He seemed to read her skepticism as clearly as he'd been able to read her body the night before.

The corners of his mouth pressed down with concern. "If you're not okay with this, Roy, I can call and find—"

He wouldn't find anybody else to come up here today. She'd have to wait weeks for a new slot. Her dreams would be on hold again.

She looked up at him. Roy. He'd called her Roy. Last night, it was her first name that he'd shouted as he was coming inside her. Now she was Roy.

Somehow, the small kindness helped.

She shook her head quickly, knowing she needed to give him an answer before he made the wrong decision.

"Okay."

"Are we okay to do this, Roy? I need to hear you say it."

This time, she found herself nodding. "We're okay."

"Relax, it'll be fun," he said, his smile wide, if a bit strained.

5

Rémy

It'll be fun.

Fun, my ass.

This was his first time sitting on a chairlift with a hard-on, and there was nothing fun about it. He was glad for the bulky ski clothes and the skis between his legs, which hid the obvious. The last thing he wanted was to make her uncomfortable—or more uncomfortable than she already was.

Damn.

Sierra was S.J. Roy, and the worst thing about it wasn't that he'd slept with her, it was that he very much wanted to do it again.

Before getting onto the chairlift, he'd outlined the plan for the day. Now, the snow still fresh after the previous evening's snowfall, was the perfect time to assess her off-piste capabilities. In the afternoon, they could go over some of the theory together and, if everything went well, she'd be ready to take the client up the following day.

If not, Rémy would take the client up, and Sierra could sign up for a four-week off-piste training session happening the following month. Though, looking at her now, he didn't think that would be necessary. She'd described her off-piste skiing as proficient in the forms she'd filled out, and Rémy knew exactly the kinds of muscles she was hiding under the ski outfit.

Stop thinking about that.

Sierra sat ramrod straight beside him. She'd scooted all the way to the end of the four-person chairlift, as if he might have some disease she didn't want to catch.

They were nearing the end of the chairlift now. Rémy felt a frisson of excitement run through him as he looked at the deep, fresh snow of the Brevent Ridge. It'd hardened a bit in the fifteen hours since, but there would still hopefully be some fresh powder for them.

He waited until she'd pushed herself off the chairlift before doing the same and sending it back down the mountain.

He skied over to the little hut and chatted with the lift attendant for a couple of minutes, letting him know where they were going. Off-piste skiing was dangerous, and Rémy wasn't about to take any unnecessary risks with Sierra's life.

Sierra was looking at him as she tightened her pole straps on her wrists, but he couldn't read her expression behind the mirrored goggles she was wearing.

"This way," he said, taking a sharp right-hand turn away from the piste and straight onto the ridge.

"Wow," she said, when he finally stopped again. "I never would have thought of going this way."

"Few people do," he confided. "Want to go first?"

"Sure," she said confidently. "Anything I need to know?"

Rémy smiled. He'd purposefully chosen a clean route, but he gave her high marks for asking the question.

"The snow is deep enough that it should be clean, but keep an eye out for hidden rocks on the left side, and make sure you stay on this side of the trees."

She nodded, confirming her understanding, checked her goggles quickly, then launched herself off the ridge. Rémy waited a few seconds before going after her.

From the way she took the first couple of turns, it was clear she knew her way around off-piste. It was there in the way she turned, applying equal weight to both skis rather than reducing the weight on the uphill ski, as she would have done on the piste. And in the way she rose and compressed on each turn, her body naturally creating that very distinctive bobbing motion that helped keep her momentum in check.

Unlike some ski instructors he'd met in the past, who were proficient but very mechanical skiers, Sierra was a creative skier. He watched her navigate an area of thin snow with ease, her technique slow and light, switching to a more aggressive stance as soon as the snow got deeper. Rémy told himself he would watch anybody the same way, but of course he knew he was lying to himself. There was something about Sierra that took his breath away.

The snow was harder than he would have expected—it must have gotten cold out here overnight, but the sun was shining, and it was a beautiful day for off-piste. He found himself relaxing and enjoying the route much more than he'd expected.

Halfway down, Sierra stopped. It was a good place to stop, and he followed suit.

"This is a gorgeous run," she said, raising her goggles to her forehead. Her face was flushed from the wind and exertion, and she was smiling.

Gorgeous.

He wasn't about to say anything inappropriate, like how much he'd personally enjoyed the view on the way down.

Suddenly, a snowboarder flew by them, passing too close to the trees. Rémy held his breath until he was gone.

"What an idiot," Sierra said, "going so close to the tree wells."

He was impressed that she knew about the danger tree wells represented, and told her as much.

"I have to admit, I have first-hand experience here. I fell into a tree well once, when I was just learning to ski. I was really lucky that I didn't get completely inverted, and I was rescued quickly, but it was one of the scariest moments of my life. So I know to avoid skiing through the trees, no matter how inviting or fresh the powder looks."

"You're right to be cautious. Tree wells are one of the main causes of non-avalanche-related snow immersion death. You'll have to stay strong on these things once you have clients asking you to do ridiculous things."

She laughed, a musical sound that he wanted to listen to again and again. "Oh, believe me, I have a lot of experience dealing with unreasonable people."

She brought out her water bottle and took a sip. Rémy watched, entranced, as the pale column of her throat bobbed up and down—remembered the way his lips had traced a path down her neck and to those high, perfect breasts ...

Stop.

Stop.

Now he was the one swallowing compulsively. He took off his backpack and brought out a handful of almonds. Pulled some into his mouth and chewed furiously.

"Is everything okay?" she asked.

Sure.

Other than the fact I can't stop thinking about you.

He nodded, still chewing—then offered her the baggie.

Sierra looked at it suspiciously for an instant. "Almonds?" Her nose wrinkled for an instant before smoothing out again. "Do you have anything chocolate?"

"Almonds provide better energy than chocolate."

Sierra's laugh echoed in the open space. "No offense against almonds," she began. "Clearly they work for you."

Rémy's body tightened under her stare. He'd never been so aware of his body before.

"But chocolate is chocolate," she continued. Her gloved fingers came up in a let-me-count-the-ways sign. "It's delicious. The perfect portable energy. It boosts immune and cardiovascular health. It contains antioxidants. And ... it's an aphrodisiac," she finished—then blushed to the roots of her hair. "Sorry. I like chocolate."

Rémy's throat had gone dry.

Stop it.

You're her instructor.

A different voice inside him spoke up, playing devil's advocate.

Only for the next couple of days.

He could survive a couple of days.

6

Rémy

Most of the time, Rémy loved his job. Few people could say they got paid to do the things they would have been doing anyway—off-piste skiing in the winter, rock climbing in the spring and summer, and lots of year-round hiking and exploring around this beautiful valley.

People who hired him, whether it was for a multi-day climbing ascent or just a few hours exploring the mountains, were usually people who loved the outdoors—people he could relate to.

In the eight years since he'd gotten his mountain guide certificate, Rémy had met some incredible people. Many of them, both clients and colleagues, he'd become friends with.

Today, just minutes after setting off for the day, he already knew that wouldn't be happening with this client.

Pompous ass.

The uncharitable thought came as a total surprise, but something about Herr Lorenz Schneider, the forty-year-old German businessman who'd hired them to ski the Vallée Blanche, simply rubbed Rémy the wrong way.

They'd met Schneider at the top of the Aiguille du Midi at nine a.m. He and Sierra had already spoken on the way, and had agreed she would be leading, and he would be introduced as an observer.

Rémy considered himself good at reading people, an ability that often came in useful for his job. As a guide, his main priority was to keep his clients safe. His second priority was to make sure they were having fun. To be able to achieve both of these objectives, Rémy had to quickly establish any discrepancy between how people saw themselves—what they'd noted in the form or interview when they set up the itinerary—and what their true abilities were. There was a bit of psychology involved in being able to do this without making them feel defensive.

Schneider had been up there already when they arrived, pacing the ice tunnel and looking impatiently at his watch. It was early enough that tourists hadn't yet started coming up in droves, so finding him was easy enough. Rémy recognized the large face, with the broad nose and deep-set blue eyes, from the picture in his file.

At six feet tall and around a hundred and eighty pounds, Schneider matched the description he'd given of himself in the reservation form. He was tanned, and looked fit—this was a man who clearly took care of his body.

He was also a walking advert for Arc'teryx, Rémy noted. He had to be wearing a cool three thousand euros worth of neon technical clothing on him.

That in itself didn't bother Rémy. Arc'teryx was a fine, if in his opinion completely overpriced, outdoor clothing brand. If his clients had money to burn, he was fine with them spending it on garish clothing, as long as it kept them warm and dry.

What did bother him was the way Schneider looked pointedly at the thick Rolex on his left wrist before walking towards them.

We're right on time.

"Call me Lorenz," Schneider had said, smiling broadly as he pumped Sierra's hand up and down, ignoring her light pained grimace. Glad for all the time spent climbing, Rémy hadn't held back when it'd become his turn to shake the man's hand, pressing until the man wore a similar grimace on his tanned face.

It was good that Sierra was taking the lead on this one. That was, of course, the whole point of the exercise, to see how she managed the client up in the mountains, and how she dealt with any issues that came up.

And, so far, she was doing great. Although Schneider had expressed an interest in doing the Grand Envers, she and Rémy had already decided before meeting him that the Petit Envers was more appropriate for his ski level and experience. He'd been ready to step in and help if Schneider became belligerent, since the man didn't seem like the kind to take no for an answer, but Sierra had artfully convinced him that he would enjoy the Petit Envers more today.

Rémy looked at the two of them standing side by side as Sierra explained some of the things they would do. Schneider said something to her in a low voice, and Sierra laughed. Rémy felt a burst of jealousy so strong, he could see it in bright Technicolor.

He clenched his teeth, not liking this new development. He didn't know what was happening to him. He wasn't a jealous man.

It was Sierra's voice that brought him back to the moment.

"Are you ready, Lorenz?" Sierra asked.

Lorenz replied with a childish cry of delight which was completely at odds with his large body and serious appearance.

Sierra looked at Rémy, waited for his nod, then launched herself into the couloir, providing a set of tracks for Lorenz to follow. Rémy closed the line.

It'd snowed again the previous evening, and this

time the powder was thick enough you could float through it. Rémy felt the usual rush of adrenaline and sense of freedom as they descended through the formidable maze of crevasses and seracs. Sierra kept her speed under control. Schneider was a very good skier, but one who hadn't spent much time off-piste. They wanted to challenge him, but not to the point of making him uncomfortable.

As they'd discussed, she stopped at the midpoint of the run, just past a large serac. Though the Petit Envers was one of the least traveled routes in the Vallée Blanche, and it was likely they'd be the only visitors today, she'd moved to the side so they would be out of the way if other skiers or snowboarders appeared.

Schneider looked around, shaking his head. For once, he seemed to be at a loss for words. Even Rémy, who was used to spending time up here, had to admit the view was spectacular. He breathed in and out deeply, enjoying the sense of serenity that could only be found out here in the mountains.

"Feel free to take some pictures, Lorenz," Sierra said. "We're not in any rush."

"It's a good time to have some water and a snack, as well," Rémy added. He brought out a handful of almonds out of his backpack, as well as some chocolate covered almonds

"Here," he said.

Her eyes eyes widened. She'd taken off her

goggles, and the blue in her eyes was lighter than he'd ever seen it before.

"You brought these for me?"

He nodded. "I know you like chocolate, Roy, but out here, almonds provide the best kind of energy."

She took the little bag almost reverently. "Thank you."

Rémy sat down on the snow beside her, leaning his back against his backpack. He had already decided he was going to ask Sierra out as soon as they got back. He'd looked at her file the previous evening, and seen this was the only training she had left before getting her certificate. It was clear to him that she was ready to become a mountain guide. Tonight, he would submit his report. Then he would ask her out.

Schneider walked around, taking videos of everything. He was going to run out of battery long before they reached the bottom if he kept this up.

"On top of the world," Schneider gushed, turning the camera three hundred and sixty degrees so it finished on a close-up of his face. "Hours away from civilization."

Rémy and Sierra shared a secret smile. The man made it seem like he'd walked for days to get here, rather than taken a cable car to the top.

When Schneider turned to include Sierra in the video, very carefully leaving Rémy out, Rémy scowled. There was that unfamiliar jealousy again. To calm himself down, Rémy walked over to the other edge, looking out onto the Chamonix valley. It was two p.m. The sun was still high, but he knew it'd get cold soon. They should keep going.

"No, don't do that!" Sierra's sharp shout had Rémy turning his head—to see Schneider standing under an overhang, doing something desperately stupid. The man still had his phone in one hand, clearly set to record. In his other hand, a ski pole, with which he started smacking the ice. Hard.

"Take a look at the incredible color of this—"

Too far away to do anything except add his own shout, Rémy watched, as if in slow motion, the snow on the overhang collapse right on top of Schneider.

It's going to bury him.

Sierra dove on top of the man. Instants later they both disappeared behind a cloud of falling ice and snow.

Rémy ran as fast as his cumbersome ski boots would allow him to, reaching them just as the snowfall cleared. He looked up to make sure no more snow was coming down—he wouldn't be of any help if he was buried under as well.

Then he saw Schneider. The man was on his side, curled into a fetal position, but he was free of the snow pile. He whimpered, which meant he was breathing.

Panic seized Rémy as he turned back towards the new mound of snow.

Sierra.

He knew how fast snow could set—it might be fist-hard when it first fell, but would turn knife-hard in a matter of minutes. He had to find her before that happened. He started at the spot where Schneider had last been standing, going down on his knees, looking for a sign, anything that might tell him where to start digging.

"Help me!" he yelled at Schneider, not waiting for the man to respond.

Slow down.

Breathe.

She's wearing a transponder.

You can find her.

He fished inside his jacket for his own transponder, switching it from transmit into receive mode.

Suddenly, his eye caught a tiny flash of red—the color of Sierra's ski jacket. He started removing snow from around it with his gloved hands. As he dug, he prayed like he'd never prayed before.

Please, God.

Please let Sierra be okay.

The flash of red grew. Though his hands were starting to hurt, Rémy didn't want to bring in the shovel and risk hurting Sierra, so he kept digging.

A flash of color shifted beside him. Schneider was sitting up and making strange, panicked sounds.

"Stop bleating and get your ass here right now, Schneider!"

Rémy turned his attention back to the snow. His digging turned frantic. And then he uncovered Sierra's face. Her hands were in front of her face—she must have placed them there when the snow fell, creating a pocket of air.

Clever girl.

"Sierra!" he shouted. He freed up her shoulders and moved her hands carefully away from her face, leaning in close to her mouth. Moments later he felt her breath, soft against his cheek.

The relief was so intense, tears came to his eyes. He rocked back on his knees.

She's breathing.

"Sierra," he said, his voice husky with emotion.

"Rémy?"

She opened her eyes and stared up at him and at the bright blue sky.

"Stay calm. I'm going to dig you out."

"What ..."

Over the next few minutes he uncovered most of her body. When he reached her legs, her mouth pulled into an agonized rictus.

Shit.

"Stop," she begged. Her eyes filled with tears, which froze on her cheek almost immediately.

"I'm sorry, Sierra, I need to get you out now."

Before the snow hardens any more.

She nodded, and he got back to work, moving slower now, not wanting to injure her further. She didn't make another sound, but tears continued to fall from her eyes.

"You're going to be okay," he said, sending out a prayer that he was telling the truth.

Finally, he'd removed enough snow that he could get her free. "I've got you," he said, leaning in towards her. He palpated her neck, her trunk and upper extremities for injuries, glad when he didn't find any.

Sierra

One hour earlier, she'd been skiing. Half an hour earlier, she'd been admiring the view with Rémy. He'd given her chocolate-covered almonds.

Where did my almonds go?

She almost giggled at the ridiculous thought. Her brain wasn't working right.

She recalled Schneider hitting the ice under the overhang. Even as she'd warned him about it, she'd known it was going to collapse. She hadn't stopped to think about it, had hurled herself at Schneider and—

Schneider.

Where's Schneider?

She turned her head, and saw him sitting down, staring at her. He looked nothing like the confident, cocky businessman they'd met up with. This man looked pale and broken. A wet patch between his legs spoke of the fear he'd lived through.

"Schneider," Rémy commanded. "Get up and bring me my backpack."

Rémy hadn't moved from her side since he'd carried her out of the hole he'd dug in the snow. She gripped his arm tight. She would beg him to stay if he tried to move away. His presence was the only thing keeping her from wailing like a baby.

She tried to move her leg—and stifled a groan.

"Where does it hurt, Sierra?"

"My knee," she gasped.

Shit.

The pain.

It didn't just hurt. It was agony. She knew cold was supposed to make things hurt less, and she certainly felt cold enough—she didn't want to know how much it would hurt under normal circumstances.

"Can you move the foot?" he asked.

Sierra nodded, working on doing just that. "I can't straighten the leg, though."

"What does it feel like?" Rémy asked softly. He turned to look behind him. "Schneider, the backpack! Now!"

"Like something's popped in my knee. Like something's burning inside."

She didn't add that the pain was making her nauseous.

"Relax, don't try to move it." He turned backwards and took the backpack Schneider offered. Schneider moved back out of her sight again.

"Is he okay?" Sierra asked quietly. She couldn't believe her client had almost died.

"He's fine," Rémy said through clenched teeth. "He has you to thank for that, Sierra."

Something warm fluttered inside her, even

though the rest of her was so cold. She liked it when he called her Roy, but liked it even better when he called her by her first name.

Rémy brought out a first aid kit from his backpack. She wondered where her own backpack was—probably under all that snow, along with her skis and Schneider's skis.

The thought cause a moment of panic before she realized it made no difference—there was no way she was going to ski down on this knee.

"Okay, I'm going to raise your ski pants and see what we're looking at," Rémy said. She'd never heard him speak so gently before.

She tried to look down, but his hands and arms stopped her from seeing anything.

"How bad is it?" she asked.

His face looked grim. "Relax. Let me take a look."

He put on a disposable glove, grabbed some snow, then turned the glove inside out, keeping the snow inside. He finished by tying a knot on it.

"What are you, some kind of boy scout?"

"They didn't teach you that in your First Aid training?" he replied lightly. He was clearly trying to distract her, and she appreciated the effort, particularly when he pressed the glove against her knee and fixed the cold pack on her with an elastic bandage.

Stars appeared in front of her eyes. She couldn't help crying out in pain.

"I'm sorry," he said soothingly, bringing her pant leg back down.

"Let me see if I can get up," she says.

He stopped it with a hand on her shoulders. "No. You'll make it worse."

"What—"

"I'm not a doctor, but I think you've torn your meniscus, Sierra." He turned around to look at Schneider. "I'm going to call and get us help."

"About time!" Schneider said belligerently. "What does this mean for us? Do we need to go back? We still have a few hours of daylight left."

Rémy sent him a glare that would have frozen a penguin. He held his phone high in the air, looking for the spot with the best reception.

"Give me a second. I'll be right back, sweetheart."

7

Rémy

He kept Sierra in his line of sight as he made the call. Instead of calling the emergency hotline, he dialed his friend Gael. Less than a minute later, he was on loudspeaker with Gael and Damien. There were sirens in the background.

Rémy quickly explained their situation.

"What's your exact location, Rémy?" Damien asked.

"We're a third of the way down the Petit Envers. We need a helicopter rescue," he repeated.

There was a long instant of silence on the phone.

"There's been a fire in the Chamonix Lodge," Gael finally said. Rémy recognized the name of the well-known hotel. "It's bad. It's affected several buildings, and multiple houses are at risk. All search & rescue helicopters are here with us."

Rémy understood what they weren't saying. Thankfully, he knew a lot of people in Chamonix.

"I'll call one of the tour companies—"

"No," Damien interrupted. "All available helicopters in the valley have been commandeered to support in fighting the fire. The entire town is at risk, Rémy. If you can hold on until first thing tomorrow morning, we'll pick you up then."

"Tomorrow morning?" he shouted, then lowered his voice. "She can't wait that long, Damien." He felt himself grow stiff with fear as he remembered something else. "There's a storm coming tonight, and we don't have the right equipment to spend the night out here."

"I'm sorry, Rémy. I really am. We cannot divert any of the rescue efforts from the fire, unless you tell me her life is at risk right now."

"Tell them!" Schneider shouted. Rémy hadn't even heard him come up to him, didn't realize he was listening in on the conversation. "We need them to come for us right fucking now."

Rémy shook his head. The selfish part of him wanted to do exactly that—but he couldn't do that. He kept silent, and turned away from Schneider.

On the other side of the line, Damien sighed, the sigh of a man used to making difficult decisions. "If not, keep her as comfortable as possible, and we'll pick you up as soon as we can."

Rémy inhaled deeply, striving to keep his temper in check. He listened to the sirens going on in the background behind Damien and Gael. He knew the PGHM were the best at their jobs, and that they were simply doing the best they could in a really shitty situation.

But Sierra needs help now.

"What about other vehicles?" Rémy asked, turning things around in his mind. There was no way a snowmobile could make it up the Petit Envers, but if they could somehow get down and meet it—

"Could you spare a couple of men and snowmobiles and meet us at the bottom of the Petit Envers?"

Damien thought for a moment. "Yes. I can't divert the helicopters, but Gael and Drake could head over in snowmobiles. What are you thinking, Rémy?"

A plan started to form in his mind. "I'll get Sierra down. Meet us in ... four hours."

"Are you sure, Rémy? How are you going to—"

"I'll figure it out."

"Copy that, Rémy. We will be there."

Rémy thanked his friends and disconnected the call.

"What are you doing? Call them back," Schneider wined. "You need to get me home. Then you can come back for her, with the rescue team."

Rémy answered in a soft voice. He didn't want Sierra to hear this conversation. "Did you even say thank you to her? She saved your life."

"I will," Schneider said quickly. "I will. I'll send

her some flowers. But I need you to get me down now. That's what I'm paying you for."

Rémy didn't bother hiding any of the disdain he felt at that moment. "Let me make one thing clear to you, Herr Schneider. I'd much rather leave you here, than leave her here. So either you help me, or you walk down on your own."

"You wouldn't dare leave me here," Schneider stammered. "It'd be the end of your career."

"Want to try me?"

Schneider blanched, making Rémy regret his harsh words. Schneider had been thrown in a situation for which he was completely unprepared. His reaction was understandable. But Rémy had to find a way to get him to cooperate.

He held the man's stare. Schneider looked away first, and so it was decided.

We're walking down.

"Let's go" Rémy said, softening his voice. "Everything's going to be okay, Schneider. You'll sleep in your own bed tonight."

He hoped he was telling the truth.

He walked back to Sierra. Though she was doing her best to hide it from him, her face was tight with pain.

"How are you feeling, Roy?" he asked. He brought out two paracetamol and put them in her hand, holding the water bottle up so she could swallow them. He didn't think the tablets would come close to making a dent in her pain, but he didn't have anything stronger to give her.

"Thank you." She swallowed them quickly, then held on to his sleeve. Her throat bobbed up and down. "Do you have a flashlight?"

"A flashlight?"

She looked down, as if ashamed of herself. "I ... I know you have to go, but I don't like the dark so much," she finally admitted. "When night comes, I—"

Understanding dawned on him. She thought he was going to leave her stranded up here, and she wanted him to know she understood.

"It's okay," she went on. Her gaze connected with his. "I know you have to get Schneider down. And I heard enough of your conversation to know the helicopter wont be here until tomorrow ..."

He swallowed thickly.

"I'm not leaving you here," he growled.

"There's no way I can stand, Rémy. I'm sorry." Her hands were clenched so tight, he knew her nails must be digging deep into her palms.

"You're not going to leave us here alone!" Schneider complained loudly.

Rémy ran a hand through his pale hair. Somewhere along the way, he'd lost his woollen hat. "Nobody's leaving anyone behind. I'll carry you down."

"Don't be ridiculous," she snapped. "You can't carry me."

He didn't bother replying as he kneeled on the

floor and started emptying his pack. Anything that was non-essential, he left on the snow. Then he placed the slimmer pack on the front of his body.

"Come over here and help me, Schneider," he asked, picking up the rope. He hoped it'd be long enough. "You're going to be my assistant."

"What do you need me to do?" the man asked. He seemed to have come to terms with the fact that neither of them were going anywhere without Sierra.

"You can't do this, Rémy," Sierra repeated.

"Save your energy, Roy. This is going to hurt."

He went down on his knees before her, his back to her front. "Okay. Schneider is going to hoist you up from the back, Roy. I'm going to need you to grab on to me. Careful with her knee, Schneider."

Once Sierra's arms were over his shoulders and her weight was on his back, he instructed Schneider to pass the ends of the rope under her armpits, then over Rémy's own shoulders and back under his arms.

"What do I do now?" Schneider asked.

"Run the rope through her legs from the front. There. Around her thighs, then back around to my waist. Use that scarf to provide some padding under her legs. You ready, Schneider?"

Pulling on Sierra's arms, Rémy stood up. His hands went under her thighs to bring him against his body, giving Schneider time to work. He didn't stop even as she stifled a scream, though her pain caused an ache in the center of his chest. He knew her pain would settle once she was firmly against him.

Every step Rémy took was agony. Sierra clenched her teeth so hard she was sure one of her fillings was going to pop.

As he stumbled in the snow one more time, then righted himself, Sierra bit her lip to stop herself from shouting out loud.

Rémy seemed to feel it anyway, and his shoulders tensed.

"I'm sorry," he gasped, but he didn't slow down.

"It's okay." A part of her wanted to ask him to stop and put her down, but she didn't think either of them would have the courage to start again if they did that.

She was amazed at Rémy's strength and stamina. The man was unflappable—carrying an unstable load on his back, in deep snow. Sierra estimated they'd been going for over an hour now. He should have given up long before now, but he hadn't, and she knew, deep in her heart, that he would get her home safe—no matter what.

Behind him, Schneider complained loudly, even though he had it relatively easy, since he was following in the tracks Rémy was creating with his boots.

"At least he's keeping us entertained," Rémy said in a low voice. His breaths were coming in harsher now, testament to the hard work he was putting in.

"He's lucky there aren't any tree wells here," she whispered against his neck.

Rémy chuckled darkly. "Why? You think I would push him into one?"

"I don't know, you tell me."

After a few minutes of silence, Rémy spoke again. "You're doing great, Sierra. We'll be in the hospital in no time—they'll take care of your leg there."

Sierra didn't say anything, but leaned her head against his shoulder and held on tight. Despite the pain, she felt safe with Rémy.

8

Rémy

Finally, she'd fainted.

Rémy sighed in relief.

God, her pain had been hard to bear.

Rémy looked at his watch. It was four p.m. He'd been walking for more than two hours, and they were only half-way down. They were going to be late to the pick-up point if he didn't get his ass in gear.

It was hard going, harder even than he'd imagined. As strong and fit as he was, trekking in deep snow with a hundred and thirty pounds strapped to his back was taking a toll on his knees.

Behind him, Schneider bitched for the twentieth time about losing his new pair of skis. He kept insisting he'd send search & rescue up for them the next day.

Rémy smiled, but didn't say anything. He'd love to be a fly in the room when Schneider ran that idea by Damien and his team.

Good luck with that.

He stumbled, and almost fell to his knees. Behind him, Sierra moaned in pain.

Rémy righted himself and forced himself to speed up his pace, willing Schneider to keep up. Sierra needed a hospital and, on top of that, temperatures were falling fast. For now, Rémy wasn't worried about Schneider or himself, with the exercise they were putting in, but Sierra was a different matter. He hoped his body would do a good enough job keeping her warm.

As time went on, putting one foot behind another became a task that took his full focus. Behind him, Schneider huffed and puffed, but he was holding up better than Rémy had expected.

He looked back when he realized he didn't hear anything behind him anymore. Schneider was on his hands and knees. "Stop," Schneider panted. "We need to stop."

Rémy backtracked to him.

"You're doing well, Schneider. Really well," he said, in what he hoped was an encouraging tone. "I need you to hold it together a little bit longer."

"I can't. I really can't."

Shit.

What do I do if he won't keep going?

"Wait. Do you hear anything?" Rémy asked.

The man huffed and puffed. "Of course I don't hear—yes! Yes! I hear it!"

Rémy saw them, then, two snowmobiles coming towards them at full speed, one of them dragging an empty stretcher in the back.

Schneider, who hadn't been able to walk a single step minutes earlier, leaped to his feet and started running down the hill, waving his arms like a man possessed. "Here! We're here!"

Rémy watched Gael ride up to him. Weak with relief, he locked his knees to keep from falling face-first in the snow.

"Jesus, Rémy," Gael said, leaping from the snowmobile.

"I couldn't leave her up there, Gael," Rémy said, falling onto his knees so Gael could untie Sierra from his back. He bit his lip to stop himself from crying out when the tension was released from the rope around his shoulders. He knew he was going to have mad rope burns on his shoulders and around his middle— hoped the scarf Schneider had placed around Sierra's thighs had protected her somewhat.

Sierra cried out as Gael picked her up.

"Careful with her knee," Rémy begged as his friend placed her on the snowmobile stretcher. Sierra moaned but didn't fully wake up, and for that Rémy was glad.

Drake shouted at them from the other snowmobile. "I've got the other package. We'll meet you at the hospital."

"I don't envy Drake," Rémy said, his lips curling up in a wry smile. "That idiot's going to spend the whole trip trying to convince him to go up for his skis tomorrow."

"*Le deseo buena suerte,*" Gael said. Rémy often forgot his friend was Mexican, until he came up with phrases in his native language. "I wish him good luck. Drake and I are going straight back to the fire as soon as we drop you off."

"Thank you for coming, man. I can't tell you—"

"You don't have to thank me, Rémy. There, I've tried to make her as comfortable as possible. Jump on, and let's get out of here."

9

Sierra

She woke up as something pinched her arm hard. The pain stopped as suddenly as it'd started. Sierra looked down to find a tube running out of her arm.

"*Desolé*, Mademoiselle," the man she assumed was a nurse said. "*Restez calme, s'il vous plaît.*"

Stay calm.

Sure.

The bed—no, not a bed, she was lying on a stretcher—moved. She looked at the wall right behind the nurse. She was in an ambulance. She'd been in one once before, when she'd knocked herself out during an ice skating competition as a child—her last ice skating competition, before she'd finally admitted to her parents how much she hated the sport.

The vehicle took a turn, and the constant throbbing in her leg shifted to agony.

"You're going to be okay, Sierra," a deep voice said. Sierra turned her head to her other side, already knowing who was sitting there.

Rémy looked exhausted. She didn't remember much from the trip down the mountain, just bits and pieces, but she knew how far from help they'd been when the accident had happened. If they were in an ambulance now, that meant Rémy had carried her all the way down.

She wanted to say thank you, but the words seemed so inadequate. But there was something important, something she should—

"Where's Schneider?" she asked, remembering.

"In another ambulance, thankfully," Rémy groaned. "He's going to be fine. He's just going to the hospital as a precaution. I don't think I could have taken one more minute of his blabbing about his lost skis."

Sierra closed her eyes for a moment, remembering Schneider's brand new Rossignol Experience skis. She'd wondered at the time if he'd bought them just for this trip. "It was a lovely pair of skis."

Rémy seemed relieved that her memory, at least, was intact.

"Have you experienced any memory loss, Sierra?"

the man she now realized must be a paramedic asked, touching the back of her head gently.

She shook her head. "I didn't hit my head, if that's what you're thinking. I just blacked out during … during the descent."

Rémy held her hand. "She was in the snow for less than a minute," he said.

Sierra's thighs were killing her. She now knew that must be from the rope seat he'd wrapped around her body. She didn't want to think of how much Rémy's shoulders were hurting.

The paramedic shone a light into her eyes.

"You don't seem to have a concussion, but I'd recommend keeping you under observation for the night. I gave you something to relax. We'll be at the hospital in a few minutes."

Sierra must have dozed off, for when she opened her eyes again they were wheeling her out of the ambulance. She looked around, suddenly panicked, looking for Rémy.

"I'm right here," he said, from the head of the stretcher. "I'm not going anywhere, sweetheart."

After what seemed like hours of being prodded and poked, she was transferred to a bed and wheeled into a small hospital room. The only other pieces of furniture were a visitor's chair and a small folding table.

"The doctor will be by to see you soon, Miss Roy," the nurse said.

Sierra tried her best to stay awake, but the doctor's definition of shortly didn't match with hers. Eventually, she found herself drifting off, thinking they must have given her some of the good painkillers this time around.

When she woke up next it was dark, and Rémy was snoring lightly in the chair beside her bed. How he'd managed to fold his large frame into that ridiculous piece of furniture, and then fall asleep on it, was a mystery.

She took her time to look at him, in a way she hadn't dared to do since ... since they'd spent the night together in his place. Before she'd known he was going to be her off piste instructor. She pulled her thoughts back quickly—she didn't want to think about the training, or about her derailed mountain guide certificate. That certainly wasn't going to happen today, and whether it happened at all depended a lot on what news the doctor shared— assuming he ever showed.

Rémy's expression was smoothed out by sleep, but he looked haggard and tired. He was still wearing the same ski pants he'd worn up on the mountain, but he'd taken off the jacket and was just wearing a black T-shirt underneath. The beginning of a beard grew on his handsome face, a couple of shades darker than his white blond hair.

His eyes opened, as if he sensed she was awake. He straightened his back in the chair.

"Thank you," she said, before he could say anything.

"You don't have to thank me, Sierra."

"You dug me out of the snow with your bare hands, and then carried me for hours in the steepest terrain imaginable, when we both know it would have been safer for you to leave me up there and come back for me later. I think it's fair to say thank you."

"I wasn't going to leave you up there."

"Are you sure Schneider's okay?"

"He's fine. He wanted to stay overnight, but the hospital staff is busy helping victims from the fire up in the mountains. Let's just say they didn't have much patience for Schneider's antics. He wants his money back for the trip, by the way. I told him he'd be lucky if you didn't sue him for endangering our lives."

"I'm not going to sue him," she said quickly.

"I figured. But let him stew on that overnight."

"You're cruel," she said, smiling. She tried to move her butt, and inhaled sharply at the resulting pain in her leg.

So much for the good stuff.

Rémy tensed. "Can I call anyone for you, Sierra?"

"Please don't," she said quickly. The last thing she wanted was one of her parents here. "I'm okay to make my own medical decisions."

"If you're sure."

"I'm sure," she said, then hesitated. "Do you have to leave?" she asked.

He shook his head. "Sleep, now, I'll be right here when you wake up."

It was late morning by the time the doctor came

around. "I'm Dr. Daniels, Miss Roy. I'm sorry I couldn't come earlier."

She detected a faint smell of smoke around him. He must have been helping out with the fire victims.

"That's okay, Doctor. I understand."

Dr. Daniels looked at Rémy, then at her again. "It's okay. Rémy is a friend. He can stay."

"I won't sugarcoat this, Miss Roy. You have a Grade 3 meniscus tear in your left knee."

"What does that mean, exactly?" she asked.

"A Grade 3 tear requires surgery."

"Surgery ..." Sierra felt tears build behind her eyes. She'd been so close to getting her mountain guide certificate and starting her new life.

"Left untreated, it's likely the meniscus could come loose and slip into the joint, leading to all kinds of complications."

"What happens after the surgery?"

Please tell me I'll be able to hike and ski again.

She didn't know what she'd do if not.

"Luckily, knee surgery has improved a lot in the last decade. We'll go in with an arthroscope. It's minimally invasive. If everything goes well, you should be starting physical therapy one week after the surgery."

"Will I be able to hike and ski again?"

"There are no guarantees in my line of business, Miss Roy, but if the surgery goes well, and we don't find anything unexpected, I see no reason why you wouldn't be able to return to your normal activities eventually, Miss Roy."

That's a lot of ifs.

Her heart sank.

"But we do need to get the surgery scheduled as soon as possible. I've already spoken with my trauma team, and we can fit you in this afternoon if you agree."

She nodded, relieved.

"Thank you, doctor."

"The nurse will bring you the consent forms to sign. Let her know if the pain gets worse. There's no reason for you to be in pain today."

The doctor left. Rémy moved closer to her bed and took her hand in his. The gentle touch felt more intimate than anything she'd ever felt before.

"You think he's telling the truth?" Sierra asked, striving to keep the fear out of her voice.

"About the diagnosis, you mean?"

Her lips curled up in a smile. "No. About being able to ski again."

"I think he's telling the truth, sweetheart. The trauma department in this hospital is topnotch, and Dr. Daniels is one of the best."

She sighed softly. "I just feel so ... helpless. I was so close to finishing the training and now—"

"Relax, Roy. The mountain guide certificate will be waiting for you when you're ready."

She looked down at her hands. She'd felt on top of the world just that morning, and now it felt as if that world was crumbling. She was sure she'd hit rock bottom—then the door opened again and her mother floated into the room.

You just never know.

Rémy

He could see the fear in Sierra's eyes—felt also how hard she was working to hide that fear, from him and from the rest of the world.

His hand gripped hers as tightly as he dared. He didn't want to cause her any pain.

You're not alone.

He cleared his throat to speak, just as the door opened and a woman waltzed inside. She closed the door behind her, walking straight to the bed.

Though he'd never seen her before, Rémy knew immediately who she was. The woman was about the same height as Sierra and had Sierra's dark blue eyes and fair skin. Under the thick layer of make-up she was wearing, he was sure he'd find the same freckles.

Then Sierra spoke, and dispelled any doubt.

"*Maman*?" she asked in a small voice. "I thought you were in Paris. What are you doing here?"

"Sierra Janine Roy!" the woman said shrilly. "What are *you* doing here is a better question."

"I fell skiing, and hurt my knee." Sierra warned him with her eyes not to say anything.

"And you didn't think of calling me?" Rémy

wondered if the shrill tone was the woman's usual voice. As if she could read his mind, the woman's eyes shifted to where Rémy was still holding on to Sierra's hand. Her lips curled up in a delicate sneer. Rémy held on. He wouldn't let go unless Sierra did so first.

Sierra sighed. "I was going to call today, as soon as I knew more. How did you—"

"Rosa came in to clean early this morning, and said it looked like you hadn't slept there. My assistant spent all morning on the phone trying to find you."

Her assistant?

Could this woman be any more insufferable?

"I'm sorry, *Maman*. I didn't want to worry you. It's okay. I'm having surgery this afternoon and—"

"*Here*?" Rémy had to stop himself from covering his ears with his hands. "You're planning on having surgery here, in this backwater? No, Sierra. Just *no*."

"Chamonix has a great trauma team, *Maman*. It's going to be okay."

"I'll call your father. We'll get an ambulance to take you back to Paris and schedule—"

"No!" Sierra looked like she was close to tears, but her voice was determined. "I am an adult, and I'm staying here, *Maman*."

The woman inched even closer, until her skinny jeans were touching the foot of Sierra's hospital bed.

"But ... but you can't stay here alone. What will you—" Watching her flail, Rémy felt the first bout of sympathy for the older woman.

"She won't be alone, *Madame* Roy," Rémy interjected, straightening to his full height.

The woman looked back at their joined hands, as if she'd only just seen them.

"And who are *you*, exactly? What do you want from my daughter?"

"Rémy Billecart. I'm a member of the *Compagnie des Guides de Chamonix*." He decided not to answer the woman's second question, lest he say something he'd later regret.

"A mountain guide," Sierra's mother spat out. "You're the reason my daughter's lying there, you're the reason she—"

"Stop. Please stop, *Maman*. You're embarrassing me!" Sierra cried out. "Rémy helped me. He's the one who brought me down from the mountain when I got hurt."

That seemed to take the wind out of her mother's sails.

"Please come home with me, Sierra. Your father and I will take care of you. We'll find the best doctors."

"I can't, *Maman*. Not this time. I have to do this my way, and I'm choosing to stay here. Go home, and I'll call you tonight, alright?"

"Fine. I'll leave. Call me back when you're ready to be reasonable, Sierra."

Sierra breathed a sigh of relief when the door closed behind her mother.

"So. That's my mother," she said. "You probably want to run for the hills."

Rémy laughed. "Not really. All families have their issues. Clearly she's one of yours." His hand pushed back a strand of hair that had fallen over her face. "I meant what I said, Sierra. You won't have to go through this alone."

10

Sierra

The doctor had told her she'd be able to go home the morning after the surgery. She just hadn't realized at the time how helpless and drugged up she'd feel.

She sat on the edge of the bed, exhausted by the effort of having dragged herself to the bathroom and back in her crutches. She inhaled and exhaled sharply, feeling like she'd just run a marathon.

Tears filled her eyes, and she wiped them away angrily.

Get ahold of yourself before Rémy comes back.

After going home to take a shower, Rémy had come back and spent the night with her once again. He'd fluffed up her pillow for her, had refilled her water, called the nurse for her when she needed to go to the bathroom ... She'd only just convinced him to go to the cafeteria to get some breakfast for himself.

But now it was time to let him go back to his life.

And you need to get on with yours.

Dr. Daniels walked in. "How are you feeling this morning, Sierra?"

She eyed the crutches beside the bed. "I still can't put any weight on my leg."

The doctor nodded. "And you shouldn't, at least for the next few days. That's what the crutches are for. Particularly now, with the snow, we don't want to risk you falling. We'll keep you on two crutches for a few days, then move you to one crutch, until you start rehab."

Sierra nodded. As much as she hated the crutches, she'd do whatever she had to do to heal. She'd be a model patient. She'd—

She forced herself to tune in to what Dr. Daniels was saying.

" ... was a success. The tear affected both the lateral and the medial meniscus, so it's good we went in now. You're young, and fit, so there's every expectation that you'll be able to heal quickly."

"How soon can I start rehab?" she asked.

"Well, let's see how things go. Today is Tuesday. I'd like to see you again on Friday. We'll see how the swelling is doing, then, and talk about next steps. Do you live alone, Sierra?"

Rémy's deep voice cut in before she could say

anything. "She won't be alone. She can stay with me for a few days. I live in a ground floor apartment, so there aren't any stairs to worry about."

Sierra hadn't even heard him come into the room. A part of her felt faint with relief. The thought of going back to the enormous house and navigating those sets of stairs was almost more than she could bear. But she also didn't want to be a burden. She wanted Rémy to see her as a desirable woman— someone he wanted in his life, and in his bed. Not ... this.

"That would certainly make me feel better, Sierra," Dr. Daniels said, as if sensing her indecision. "You shouldn't be putting any stress on the knee as it heals —particularly during the first few days."

"Anything else, Doctor?" Rémy asked.

The doctor laughed. "We've been through this several times, you and I, I think. Just remember RICE —rest, ice, compression and elevation. Okay, if that's settled, I'll sign the discharge papers and get a nurse in here to help you get dressed, Sierra, so you can leave."

Sierra balanced on her good foot. She realized she'd left the crutches too far away, but Rémy reached over and brought them to her.

"What did he mean, when he said you've been through this several times?"

"I've never torn my meniscus, but I've been in Daniels's care several times. He fixed my collarbone last year."

"And who did you go home with?" she asked.

Rémy laughed. "I stayed with Gael for a few days. You probably don't remember him, he's the guy who drove the snowmobile."

"Are you sure this is okay, Rémy?" She wrung her hands with indecision. Maybe she should swallow her pride and call her parents. Her mom would be only too happy to arrange for a full-time nurse to stay with her.

"It's fine, Sierra. I told you I wanted a chance to get to know you better, didn't I?" He raised his hands. "Hey, don't look at me like that, this isn't what I had in mind, but I'm still not going to waste the chance. You need help, Sierra, and I'm happy to give it, just like you would if our roles were reversed."

Sierra nodded slowly. "I *am* grateful. Please don't think I'm not."

"So what's wrong? Out with it, Sierra."

"I ... I'm scared."

Rémy took a step back as if she'd slapped him. "Of me?"

"No," she said quickly. "Not of you. You said the training would be waiting for me, for when I was ready."

"Yes."

"What if I'm never ready? That's what scares me. What if I'm never able to—"

"Sweetheart, you had surgery twelve hours ago. Give your body a chance to recover." He took her in his arms, and she felt her fears slowly ebb away.

11

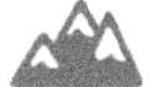

Rémy

The week Sierra had spent in his house had been torture. Rémy had spent those days with a permanent case of blue balls, unable to even take care of it himself because the walls between the living room and bedroom were paper thin, and he hadn't want her to hear.

It'd gotten so bad that she'd even commented on his grouchy mood on the third morning, offering to give him back the bed and take the couch herself. He didn't remember what he'd growled back in reply, but she hadn't asked again.

He should be happy she was back in her own place now, and engaged in physical therapy—except he wasn't. He missed her. He missed her dreadfully.

He hadn't even changed the bed sheets after she'd moved out, because he could smell her on the bed and it made him feel less lonely.

Lonely.

He might as well admit it. Even though he'd been on his own since he was seventeen, and couldn't remember ever feeling lonely before, in just a short few days he'd gotten used to coming home and spending time with Sierra in the evening.

Every day, he'd seen her get a little bit stronger. He'd been impressed by the discipline with which she'd followed the doctor's recommendations, alternatively icing and elevating her leg, then later on wearing the brace as needed.

He'd found out more things about her—that she loved Thai food, that she could bake a mean cake with just five lousy ingredients, that she sang in the shower when she thought nobody was listening. Everything he learned about her made him want to get to know her better.

He hadn't touched her in a sexual way since that first night together. At first, she hadn't been feeling well, so he'd felt like a bastard for even thinking about her that way. But he couldn't help it if, every time he saw her, he was reminded of how responsive she'd been in his arms. He wanted her so much he could hardly think straight.

Last night, she'd clearly been feeling better. She'd sat down beside him on the couch to watch TV and scooted closer and closer to him—close enough that he'd been able to smell that fresh, spicy scent that was just her.

In case he hadn't been getting the hint, she'd leaned over so the side of her breast touched his arm. Warmth flowed into his body from their touch. The pull had been electric and irresistible—except, when he'd turned around to kiss her, he'd jostled her leg and made her cry out in pain.

Cursing, he'd jumped up and off the couch, generating as much space between them as possible.

"I'm sorry."

"Don't be. Please come back, Rémy."

"No. Not until you're healed."

"But I want you tonight."

"We can wait."

"Can we?" she'd asked, pointedly staring at his crotch, which sported a sizable hard-on.

He'd laughed wryly. "This? I've been walking around like this for days, sweetheart."

"And wouldn't you like to do something about it?"

"Yes. As soon as you're feeling better."

Huffing lightly, she'd gone back to her movie, and he'd gone off to take yet another cold shower. In the morning, he'd dropped her off at her physical therapy appointment. He'd known she'd be getting a ride with her colleague Celine afterwards, and heading back to her own place, rather than his, but he hadn't expected his place to feel quite this empty.

Sitting down to a lonely meal of Thai leftovers, he picked up his phone and typed in a message.

How are you feeling? I miss you.

He deleted it before sending, then tried again.

How did the session go this morning?

That was safer, and besides, she might need to vent. He knew how much of a bitch rehab exercises could be.

He held his breath when she started typing in return.

Good. Painful. But better than yesterday.

I'm glad. Did you see Dr. Daniels?

Not today.

I wish you'd stayed a few more days. I can come pick you up if you need anything.

Her response came a bit slower now.

Thank you, Rémy. For everything. But my parents have come to stay for a few weeks, and it would hurt their feelings if I don't stay with them.

Shit. He hoped her mother had gotten over herself in the week since they'd met.

I understand. The offer stands if you need anything.

Thank you. Goodnight.

Goodnight, sweetheart.

Sierra

Rehab sucked—but it also worked, apparently.

Sierra had been through so many conflicting feelings in the last five weeks, it was difficult at times to wrap her head around them. She'd gone from absolute panic at the thought that she'd never be able to walk again, lets alone ski and run, to elation whenever she reached a new milestone in rehab, then back to panic again. And so on, multiple times.

Today, however, was different. Today she was graduating from her official rehab program. She'd still get to see Marguerite, her therapist, once a week, to continue rebuilding the muscle strength she'd lost after the accident, but she'd been cleared by Dr.

Daniels to restart her regular exercise routine—walking and running and skiing, as long as she started slowly.

They'd been very clear on the word *slow*.

She felt like hopping all the way back to her car, but knew that might be the easiest way to find herself back in Marguerite's care.

You need to be careful.

You've worked too hard to undo it all now.

She wished she could tell her parents in person, but they'd left for Paris a few days earlier. She'd send them a quick message as soon as she got home. After her initial ranting and raving, her mother had done everything she could to help Sierra's recovery, as had her father. It didn't escape Sierra's notice that the two of them, who hated snow and usually never set foot in Chamonix before spring, had chosen to spend almost a month here this winter.

The other person she wanted to tell was Rémy. Though they hadn't seen each other much in the weeks since she'd left his place—and, when they had met up, he'd been determined to keep his hands off her—they'd texted or spoken almost every night. He was adventurous, and sexy, and caring, and almost everything Sierra could have wanted in a man.

She never consciously made the decision, but her legs took her towards Rémy's apartment. It was a beautiful day for a walk—one of those late February days that make you think of spring already. Her knee felt tight at the start of the walk, but there was no pain, and that alone felt like cause for celebration.

Rémy opened the door as soon as she knocked. His gray eyes widened as they saw her. "Is everything okay, Sierra?" he asked worriedly.

She looked him up and down, speechless for a moment. He was barefoot and shirtless, dressed in just a pair of jeans that seemed to hold on to his slim hips as if by magic. She hadn't forgotten how lean and strong he was, but to see him like this—it literally made her mouth water and something heat up inside her.

"Sierra?"

"I'm okay. Everything's okay. I graduated from the rehab program today," she mumbled, then shook herself. "Why are you naked?"

His eyes twinkled with amusement. "I'm not naked. I had a shower and was getting dressed when you knocked on my door."

"Maybe you should finish getting dressed," she said. "Unless you want to give me ideas," she said bravely.

Please give me ideas.

He led her inside but didn't make any move to touch her.

"Give me a minute. Make yourself comfortable. I'll go find a T-shirt."

Ouch.

The rejection stung.

She decided to sit down on the couch to wait.

Everywhere she looked around his apartment, she was reminded of the way he'd cared for her that first week after surgery, when she'd felt helpless and hadn't known if she'd ever get her life back. He'd wanted her then, she was sure, even though he'd held back from touching her.

So why doesn't he want me now?

Tears rose to the back of her eyes but she willed them back. She wasn't going to cry in front of him.

"I spoke to the guides association earlier this week, Sierra," Rémy said, coming back. He looked great in a slim, dark gray T-shirt, the same color as his eyes, but she missed the view of his muscled chest.

"You did?" she asked, nervously. She'd been planning on reaching out to them herself, but hadn't built up the courage yet. She was worried about what they would say.

"Relax, Sierra. I told you the training could wait until you were ready."

"What did they say? Tell me I don't need to take Schneider back up again," she joked weakly.

Rémy's nostrils flared. "I'm the one who couldn't face that."

"Though he did get me some lovely flowers," she said. She still remembered how weird it'd been to get flowers from the man, back at the hospital.

"The association agrees with me that your work that day on the mountain was solid. You saved a man's life, Sierra."

She wriggled uncomfortably on the couch. She

hadn't done anything anybody else wouldn't have done.

"So they're giving you credit for that day. But you still need one more training to get the off-piste skiing checked off the list." He spread a map open in front of her. "You'll be able to choose from all these routes."

Her mouth fell open. This was more than she'd hoped. "Just one route? Then I'm done?"

Rémy's thick lips parted in a smile, and he nodded. "I told you everything would be okay, sweetheart."

"Thank you, Rémy." The tears that filled her eyes this time were happy tears.

"There's no rush, either," he went on quickly. "The association has agreed to extend the validity of all your qualifications for a year, in light of what happened."

Sierra shook her head. She couldn't wait a year.

"No. I want to do it this year. I want to be working this summer."

His gaze went to the snow outside his window. "There's probably a month of good snow left. If you're ready for it within that time, I'll take you up." He sighed. "I just don't want you to get hurt again, Sierra. It was—it was hard to see you in pain."

Her heart melted a little at the admission. Maybe he wasn't as unaffected as he tried to pretend. She sidled closer to him.

"So ... we have a month, you say." She went up on tiptoes. Her mouth grazed his jaw—he tensed for a moment, and she was almost sure he was going to move away. Then his head shifted lower and his mouth was on hers, strong and urgent. Sierra pushed herself closer to him, wanting nothing between them, as their tongues fought for access to each other's mouth. She clung to him, and felt him cling back to her, felt his heart beating frantically against her ear. She moaned softly into the kiss—an instant before he broke it off.

"No," he said, running his hands along his hair. "I won't be able to stop if we do this."

"We don't have to stop," she said. "You won't hurt me."

"It's not that. Or not only that."

"Then what is it? Why don't you want me anymore?"

He growled and pushed her back into his embrace, this time grabbing on to her butt and pulling her against him.

"You think I don't want you?"

She could feel all of him now. A very female part of her rejoiced.

He wants me.

"What is it, then?"

"I need to maintain some degree of impartiality until we're back down from the mountain. I can't—I can't do *this* with you until your certification is done."

"Impartiality?" she asked. She pushed her hips into his, delighting in his ragged groan. Then she moved back and waved at the charged air around them. "There's nothing impartial about this."

"You know what I mean, sweetheart. I want you. I've wanted you for weeks. But we can wait until afterwards."

Sierra nodded. Her mouth felt dry.

"When's the next big snow expected? I'll be ready then."

13

———————

Rémy

Standing at 3,613 meters from sea level, the Col du Midi glacier was an off piste skier's wet dream. The snow from the previous evening hadn't settled yet, and the powder was fresh and pristine, the valley opening before them like a secret kingdom.

That wasn't why Rémy had chosen it, however. Rather, it was its proximity and easy accessibility to the Aiguille du Midi cable car that had guided his selection. Rémy knew Sierra had been working out for the last three weeks, and she swore her knee was as good as new, better than the other one even, but he didn't want to add an unnecessary hike to the morning of off-piste skiing.

When they were done with the descent, they'd get

back on the cable car at the lower stop and let it take them all the way back to Chamonix.

The avalanche risk plaque on the wall read 3 out of 5.

Moderate risk.

He wasn't worried. 4 would have been a concern, but 3 was to be expected at this height, and at this time of year.

"How are you feeling, Roy?" he asked, tightening the traps on his helmet. At the risk of repeating himself, he found himself telling her the same thing he'd spent weeks telling her. "I know you really want to do this, but please don't endanger your recovery. If it hurts, you—"

"Yes, yes, if it hurts I'll let you know. I know you don't want to have to carry me down, Rémy."

He frowned behind his goggles. "You know that's not what—"

"That was a bad joke. I'm sorry. Listen, I know this route, I'm feeling good, and I promise I'll let you know if that changes."

Stubborn woman.

Knowing it was as good a promise as he was going to be able to extract out of her, he signaled for her to go ahead.

His heart lodged in his throat as she disappeared into the steep pitch. He watched her for a couple turns, relaxing when he couldn't detect her favoring her left knee in any way. He leaned into his skis and followed her, letting his skis build in enough speed to navigate the deep snow.

One of the best things about off-piste skiing was that, regardless of how many times one had skied a particular route, every time felt like the first time. Since it was impossible to predict just how much snow would build up on any particular point, or how it would behave when the skis cut through it, each time was a chance for a skier to trace their own path, to find their own way forward.

He whooped as his skis plunged off a small ridge, landing easily on the ground below. He braked besides Sierra, who'd stopped to stare at him.

"Still feeling good, Roy?" he asked.

She nodded. "It's as beautiful as I remembered, up here."

They both heard the noise at the same time and look beyond the *couloir* they were on.

"What's that?" she asked quietly, instants before the two snowmobiles came in sight, traveling at full throttle across the virgin slope. Judging by the noise decibels, and the speed at which they were moving, Rémy would bet anything they'd tuned the engines to increase top speed.

"Morons. Don't they realize this is an avalanche area?"

"Hopefully it'll be ok—"

The rumbling of the mountain was the first indication that things were not going to be *okay*. It was followed by a deep thunk as icy plates the size of refrigerators tore from the mountain. The plates fell as if in slow motion, but Rémy knew just how fast the sliding snow would gather, quickly reaching speeds of a hundred and twenty kilometers per hour.

Thankfully, he and Sierra were far enough away that the avalanche wouldn't strike them, and Rémy was pretty sure the idiots who'd caused the avalanche would also be clear of the area in time.

"Oh, my God," Sierra whispered.

Sierra's fingers tightened around his arm like claws, while her other hand pointed at two colorful blobs near the middle of the slope.

Skiers.

Shit.

The skiers had obviously heard the same sound they had, but it was too late for them to do anything. They stood there, frozen, right in the path of the oncoming snow—like deer caught in the headlights.

Suddenly, Rémy's world narrowed to two colors, the color of the jackets.

"You focus on the yellow one," Rémy said urgently. "I'll take the black. We need to know where they disappear."

Sierra nodded tightly.

Thunder rolled down the mountain. Rémy clamped down on the almost ungovernable fear, focusing his full attention on the black blob as it was swallowed by the snow.

Swim.

Swim.

Rémy breathed a sigh of relief as the figure—a short man, or maybe a woman—began to kick and swing his arms in a swimming motion, striving to stay on the surface of the snow. He or she was no match for the power of the avalanche, however, and after only a few seconds he began to sink. Rémy worked to memorize the exact spot where he lost the skier.

Finally, as quickly as it'd begun, the world was silent again—as if the roaring inferno from seconds earlier had never happened at all.

"Is it safe to go out there now?" Sierra asked, her eyes fixed on the spot where Rémy assumed the figure in yellow had disappeared.

"Give it half a minute," Rémy said, looking at his watch.

Finally, he nodded. Time was of the essence. If they weren't able to dig the victims out in fifteen minutes, their chances of survival would drop catastrophically. "Let me call it in."

He brought out his phone and, without ever taking his eyes off the spot where the person in black had disappeared, dialed the emergency number and asked to be patched in with the PGHM. Less than a minute later, he hung up, sighing in relief. The search and rescue team would be here soon.

"We're each going to head to the spot where we lost our target, Roy, and plant our skis in an *X* to mark it. Then we'll regroup."

"On it," she said, already moving forward.

It wasn't easy to navigate the thick blocks of snow

on skis, but Rémy knew it'd be slower in his boots. Finally, he reached the spot where he'd lost sight of the skier. He popped out of his skis and quickly buried them in the snow in the shape of an X. Only then did he allow himself to look around him.

He'd held hope that he might be able to see a sign of the person buried underneath, but the snow around him was pristine. It was like the avalanche had never happened.

He turned down the slope to where Sierra kneeled next to her own crossed skis, digging madly.

"Do you see anything?" Rémy shouted.

"A pole! I've got a pole!"

With a silent apology to the skier lying under the snow somewhere beneath him, Rémy raced down to where Sierra was standing. By then, she'd uncovered most of the upside down pole. Rémy dug beside her until the handle appeared.

Her expression fell as she realized the pole wasn't attached to anything.

"Check for transceivers," Rémy said, his voice tight. Sierra nodded quickly, bringing hers out of an inner pocket and setting it to receive. He quickly switched his off.

He held his breath, knowing her answer could mean the difference between life and death.

Eventually, she shook her head dejectedly.

"Either they're not carrying trasceivers, or they're not set to transmit."

Hell.

Rémy took off his backpack and looked for the collapsible shovel he always carried with him. Sierra's eyes widened when she saw it.

"I need to get myself one of those." She took off her own backpack. "I've got a probe, though."

"Good, bring it out," he said. Together, they assembled the collapsible probes, which looked like thin ski poles that'd been screwed together.

"I've never … I've never had to …"

He wasn't about to lie to her, but it was important that they both keep up hope. "We have a good chance of finding them, Sierra. Let's start right here, where you found the pole."

They stood shoulder to shoulder with their legs apart, using the probe to test the snow between their feet. When they reached the ten-foot mark, they moved to the next imaginary line and tried again.

"I've got something!" Sierra shouted. "The probe's not going in."

Rémy tested the spot with his own probe. Most of the probe went in deep—then snagged on something.

Please let this not be a rock.

The object underneath the probe shifted.

"I think you found your skier, Sierra," he breathed out. He looked at his watch. The person had been under for four minutes.

"How can I help?" she asked. "I don't need a shovel. I can dig with my hands."

"Call the search & rescue team first. See how close

they are. Tell them we think we may have located one of the victims."

Leaving the probe in the snow, Rémy shifted downhill until he was one and a half times as far from the probe as the depth he estimated the victim to be buried at, and started digging into the side of the slope, towards the victim.

He prayed the hole made by the probe was near the person's face, creating a small airway.

We need more time.

He shoveled quickly and rhythmically, moving the snow out to the side rather than behind him to conserve his strength. When the snow reached his waist, he stopped and repositioned himself, allowing himself a quick look at his watch. Five more minutes had gone by.

They've been under for nine minutes.

He started digging again. It seemed to him the snow was hardening by the second. There was no time to waste.

Sierra sidled up to him.

"They'll be here in ten minutes, Rémy," she said. She'd found herself a large flat stick, and used it to remove the snow he was pushing to his side, so he could keep digging for longer before repositioning himself.

Sweat poured down his face, and he wished he'd thought to take his ski jacket off, but he didn't stop to wipe his face. Every second counted now.

"How long has it been, Sierra?" His hands were cramping around the shovel.

If he knew her at all, she'd be keeping close track of the time.

"Thirteen minutes."

Shit.

The fifteen-minute window was coming up soon.

Ignoring his burning muscles, Rémy redoubled his efforts.

They both saw it at the same time—a flash of yellow in the snow.

"There!"

Rémy set down the shovel, worried about hurting the skier. Together, he and Sierra dug frantically with their gloved hands, uncovering more of the yellow jacket, trying to identify which way the person was facing.

"I see an arm!" Sierra shouted. She scooted forward on her knees, sweeping snow away like an archaeologist before a big find. Rémy followed suit. Moments later, they'd uncovered the face and upper chest area.

It was a man. He was lying face up, thankfully, so they didn't need to move him to begin working on him.

Sierra repositioned herself next to the man's chest and lowered her mouth to his cheek.

Rémy held his own breath for a few seconds.

"He's breathing!" she said.

Rémy looked at the ski poles he'd planted further

down the hill, where another victim waited. She seemed to read his mind.

"I'll stay here with him and keep him comfortable if he wakes up."

He nodded and raced back down the hill.

A rumbling noise had him looking up—the PGHM was here. Moments later, the helicopter touched down. The noise died down as the pilot shut off the engines.

Four men and a dog stepped out, followed moments later by a red-haired woman. Rémy had never been as happy to see his friends. All of them carried shovels twice the size of the one he'd been using.

"How did you get out here so quickly?"

"We were in the area," the woman said softly. Rémy knew Kat was one of the best rescue pilots in the country.

Rémy gave them a quick situation report. The tall blond man, Jens, who Rémy knew was a doctor, ran towards Sierra.

The other men and the woman came towards him, each one carrying a probe.

Rémy looked at his watch.

"The skier's been under eighteen minutes," he explained.

Damien took charge, quickly organizing them along imaginary lines in the snow facing downhill from Rémy's crossed skis.

Sierra didn't even notice the tall, blond man until he was almost on top of her.

"Jens Melkopf," he said. "I'm a doctor with the PGHM."

She sighed. "Thank God. I'm Sierra."

She focused on sharing the facts that he needed to know, forcing the words out past the fear in her throat as the seriousness, the enormity of what had happened, started closing in on her.

"He was under for thirteen minutes. He's breathing, but hasn't regained consciousness."

The man in the snow was young. Or maybe he just looked young because he was unconscious. She didn't say anything about the lack of color in the man's face, or how much it scared her.

The doctor nodded calmly, checking the man's airway and pulse rate. As he took charge of the situation, Sierra felt herself faint with relief. She realized just how much she'd been relying on the adrenaline coursing through her veins.

From his backpack, the doctor brought out a cervical collar. He said something softly into his ear piece before addressing her again.

"Keep him steady, like this, make sure he doesn't move. He could have internal injuries. I'm going to dig him out."

The doctor took off his ski jacket and started shoveling snow in smooth, efficient moves, beginning around the man's legs.

"Doctor, he's waking up," Sierra said, speaking loudly to be heard over the shoveling snow. The doctor—Jens, he'd said his name was—rushed back up to them.

The young man started thrashing around inside the frozen coffin. Eyes the color of warm whiskey stared up at them. "How ... What ..."

"Sir, my name is Jens Melkopf. I'm with the PGHM. You've been in an avalanche. Stay calm, we're here to get you out."

"Avalanche ... Gina!"

"Is that who you were skiing with?"

At the man's nod, Jens spoke softly into his mic again.

"*La mia fidanzata,*" the young man whispered.

Sierra looked at Jens, not understanding the word.

"*Fidanzata* ... I think that's his fiancée."

"What's your name?" Sierra asked, looking to distract the man.

"Pietro." He pronounced it with a thick Italian accent. "Gina. Where's Gina?" He was getting agitated again.

"Please be calm. There's a search party looking for her." This seemed to mollify Pietro somewhat. He closed his eyes, and a tear rolled down, freezing on his pale cheek.

Sierra looked downhill for the others. At least now they knew who they were looking for.

Gina.

"Are you sure there isn't anybody else buried here?" the doctor asked Sierra.

The question made her feel physically sick.

In her mind, Sierra replayed the scene as it'd been just before the avalanche hit.

No, there hadn't been anyone else.

Just the snowmobiles, who were long gone, and the skiers.

She shook her head. "No, just one more person."

Jens nodded. "Relax, Sierra. If it's humanly possible to find them, we'll do so."

The group moved in a straight line, stopping in a coordinated fashion every couple of steps to insert the probes.

"Probe left! Probe center" Probe right! Step!"

Beside them, a beautiful black-haired dog walked in circles around them. Every so often, a handsome dark-haired man spoke gently to the dog. Sierra was too far away to hear what he said.

"Bailey can smell up to a meter under the snow," Jens said, following her line of sight. He'd gone back to digging around Pietro's body. "That's Hiro, her handler."

"Thirty minutes," Rémy announced loudly. Sierra almost buckled at the news, but the group didn't react, just kept right on searching.

Sierra held Pietro's neck still and spoke to him

softly. Her knee was killing her from kneeling on the clunky ice and snow, and had been for some time now, but now wasn't the time to worry about that.

"I have something here!" the woman said. She and one of the men began digging.

In that instant between hope and despair, Sierra held her breath.

Eventually, the woman reached down and brought out something dark.

A helmet.

Sierra knew people could often be found underneath such objects. It meant they were digging in the right area, at least.

By now, Pietro was completely out of the snow. He'd lost consciousness again, and a part of Sierra was grateful for that.

If his fiancée's not alive ...

She forcibly stopped the thought before it could solidify in her mind.

Jens palpated Pietro's body, then placed heat packs and an emergency blanket around him.

"We need to prevent further heat loss before we can get him to the hospital."

Downhill from them, the team probed carefully, moving with renewed enthusiasm.

Suddenly, the dog—Bailey—barked three times in quick succession. Her handler moved behind her and rubbed her ears, as the rest of the team began digging around that area.

From where she was standing, Sierra could see

the hole being formed. The team had spread out in a V formation, with a leader at the front, two people on one side, and two people on the other.

Figuring that the tall, broad-shouldered doctor would be more useful than she would when it came to digging, she spoke up.

"I can stay with him."

"Are you sure? Keep him still, as you've been doing, and let me know if he wakes up again."

Moments later, the leader shouted. "I see a hand!"

The team members went to their knees and began pushing at the snow with their hands. Suddenly, a woman's harrowing scream rent the air.

The red-haired woman's mouth wasn't moving, and Sierra knew she hadn't made the sound either. It took her a moment to believe what her ears and her brain were telling her.

Pietro's fiancée was alive.

Moments later, two of the figures moved away and Sierra was able to confirm that Gina was indeed alive —most of her body was still in the snow, and she was alternatively yelling, taking in huge gulps of air, then yelling again.

It felt to Sierra like she'd been drowning as well, and was only now able to draw breath. She took Pietro's hand in hers and told him the news, even though she didn't know if he could hear her.

Sometime later—she couldn't say if it was five minutes or fifteen, but Gina had already been loaded up onto the helicopter—someone came up beside her. It was the doctor.

"Good work, Sierra. We're going to take Pietro now," he said, pulling up a sled. Between him and another man, they loaded Pietro onto the sled.

Sierra stood to get out of their way—and wavered. Her knee felt like it was on fire. Suddenly Rémy was there, reaching out before she could face-plant into the snow. She leaned into him gratefully.

"I'm sorry. I'm okay."

"We can take the helicopter down, Sierra," Rémy said, but even as he spoke the rotors came to life. Kat was in the pilot's seat, getting ready for take-off.

Sierra shook her head violently. "I'm not taking the helicopter down."

She put some weight on the leg, relieved when it held. She didn't think she'd really injured herself, she'd just been in the same position for too long.

"Sierra ..." Rémy began. His jaw was clenched tight.

An imposing man with penetrating blue eyes walked up to her. "Damien Gray," he said, offering his hand. Sierra took off her glove and shook it, raising her face to look into penetrating blue eyes.

"*Commandant* Damien Gray leads the PGHM search and rescue team."

"You're not leaving with them?" she asked, surprised. Already, the helicopter was lifting off.

It was Gael who replied. "Kat and Jens are flying

straight to the hospital with Pietro and Gina. The rest of us will wait for another ride."

"Rémy told me you're getting certified as a mountain guide today, Miss Roy," Damien continued. "I will write a letter of recommendation and make sure Colonel Pelegrin signs it, to highlight your courage and ability to keep a cool head under pressure."

Sierra felt herself blushing under the man's stare.

"I appreciate it, though I really didn't do much."

"Are you sure you're going to be okay?" Gael asked. "We can drop you off at the hospital if you need somebody to look at that knee."

Rémy looked at her questioningly, making it clear the decision was hers to make.

Damien's phone rang before she had a chance to reply. He looked down at the number and quickly slid his thumb to pick up the call. Though he turned around as he did so, Sierra heard the first few seconds of the conversation. "Is everything okay? Yes, of course."

He finished the conversation quickly and turned back towards them. "Shit. I need to get down. My son fell at school and hit his head. They think he's okay, but—"

His blue eyes were narrowed in worry now. He looked at the sky, as if he could materialize a helicopter out of thin air. And, suddenly, there it was, a second helicopter, heading towards them.

"Please go," she said quickly. "We're good to ski down."

"Thank you. We'll call you later," Damien told Rémy.

When the noise of the second helicopter died down, the mountain felt strangely silent and empty. Rémy pulled her gently to the ground on top of his jacket. He placed some chocolate-covered almonds in her hand, much as he'd done the last time they'd been skiing.

"Here. Eat something."

"Where did you get these?"

"Do you like them?"

She laughed, feeling the strength return slowly to her body. "I love them."

"Good."

They sat in silence for a few minutes.

"Do you think Gina and Pietro are going to be okay?"

"Jens seemed to think so, and I trust him."

"What about Damien's son?"

"I'm sure he'll be fine. Damien doesn't have it easy, though. The boy's mother isn't in the picture, and with his job—"

"These people ... they are all your friends," she said. A statement, not a question.

Rémy nodded. "Gael is my best friend, but they are all good people. A great team. You've met Damien, Gael, Jens, Kat, Hiro ... and Bailey, of course. There's also Drake. He's Damien's second-in-command. You might remember him, he's the one who took

Schneider down. He must have been off today, otherwise he would have been here as well."

"I don't remember him. I must have been pretty out of it that day," she mumbled.

Then Sierra asked the question that had been on her mind.

"Gina was under the snow for over thirty minutes. How did she survive?"

Rémy considered for a moment. "She was swimming against the snow as she went under. That movement may have created the air pocket that saved her life." He shrugged. "Somehow, she got lucky."

Sierra pondered that for a few more minutes. Luck, an air pocket, a miracle, whatever they wanted to call it, Gina had survived.

"We should go down."

"Are you sure you're feeling up to it?"

"I need you to sign that certificate tonight, remember?"

"Jesus, Sierra, is that why you didn't want to go in the helicopter? You know you've—"

"No," she said, shaking her head. "It just wouldn't have felt right. I want to ski down. I need to."

Rémy nodded, his expression filled with understanding. His eyes were the same color as the laden sky.

"Come on," he said, pulling her up gently. "Let me get your skis."

She followed Rémy down the route. Half-way down to the cable car, he cut onto the piste. She knew he was trying to make it easier on her knee, and she was grateful. They got on the cable car and rode back down into town in silence.

As they left the cable car, Rémy took her skis from her and lifted them easily onto his shoulders.

"Do you need to go to the hospital?" Rémy asked. "My car is right there."

Sierra shook her head. "I'm okay. I just need to ice it a bit."

"I can give you a ride home."

Normally, she would have said no. She didn't like anybody to see her parents's house. It always led to too much explaining. But Rémy had already met her mother, and he hadn't run yet.

"That would be great. Head towards Les Houches, for now, if you can."

14

———

Rémy

Rémy drove carefully, avoiding any sudden turns. Out of the corner of his eye he could see, by the stiff way Sierra sat, just how much pain she was in.

He passed Les Houches, asking her for further directions. They were entering an area of Chamonix he'd never had reason to visit before. There were no apartment buildings here, no semi-detached homes. The properties he could see from the road were so large, in fact, it was often impossible to see the houses behind the large, ornate gates.

What the hell?

"Take the next right, Rémy," she said softly.

Rémy did as she asked, entering a paved driveway. Beyond lay a solid gate, as large or larger than the ones they'd just passed. Rémy read the sign engraved by the door.

Chalet de Cristal.

Sierra pushed a button on her key fob and the gate opened slowly. The trees lining the driveway seemed to lean towards them as he drove through.

"This feels ... secluded," he said carefully.

As they approached the house, the trees gave way to a manicured lawn surrounding the paved driveway. They passed a couple of buildings that he assumed were also part of the property. The floorspace of each looked substantially larger than that of his apartment.

At the end of the driveway, the main house awaited—a large, two-floor structure, made of glass and wood and stone.

Rémy stopped the car, then turned to look at her.

"I don't suppose your father's the *chauffeur*, right?" he joked.

"My parents don't have a driver," she said, without a trace of irony.

He thought back to his own small one bedroom apartment, wondered what it must have felt like to her when she'd stayed with him.

Like a sardine can, probably.

She was looking at him with a worried—almost frightened—expression on her face. And he realized, then, that she expected him to leave her there and take off.

"Come on, Roy," he said, not trusting himself to call her by her first name. "Let's get you inside."

She'd already opened the car door by the time he got around to the passenger seat, but he leaned into the car and put one arm under her knees, the other one around her back, picking her up easily, delighting in how she pressed herself against him.

"Where are the keys?"

"No keys, it's a biometric door."

He watched, feeling like an idiot, as she pressed her index finger to a small panel on the side of the door. The heavy, wooden door opened silently, letting them into the house.

He started at the life-sized terracotta Xion warrior presiding over the entrance hallway.

"Which way?" he asked quietly, walking past the sculpture. Sierra pointed towards what he assumed was the living room. Rémy's eyes went immediately to the large bay windows and, beyond that, the mountains.

Everything in the house seemed over-sized, from the high-vaulted ceilings and floating fireplace to the enormous oak and stone dining table and, beyond that, the steel-lined kitchen that wouldn't look out of place in a restaurant.

Everything except for Sierra, who seemed to have grown smaller in his arms. He set her down gently on a beige extra-long sofa.

Numerous art pieces strewn around the room— including paintings, sculptures and random artifacts kept inside thick glass boxes—made the place feel more like a museum than a home.

"Thank you, Rémy. I'll be okay, you don't have to stay."

"I'll get you a painkiller," he said, ignoring her. "Where do you keep your medicines?"

"First aid box, in the ski room. Down those stairs, on the ground floor."

A fucking ski room.

"I'll be right back," Rémy said, keeping his expression neutral.

He took the stairs three by three down to what she'd referred to as the ground floor. He understood why once he reached the lounge area below. Since the house was built on several levels, the lounge faced a garden with a large oval pool, now frozen.

The ground beneath his feet creaked. He looked down to discover frosted glass flooring and, underneath, something that looked like—

You've got to be shitting me.

It's a hydraulic floor.

There was an indoor pool underneath the lounge floor. Shaking his head at the absurdity, Rémy left the lounge and walked down a corridor, passing a laundry room, a guest bedroom, a linen cupboard and, finally, the ski room.

A couple of minutes later he had two painkillers in hand. He stopped by the enormous kitchen for an ice pack, and was back at Sierra's side a minute after that.

She was leaning forward on the couch, both hands grabbing at her knee, as if she could make the pain go away. She let go as soon as she saw him.

"Here. Take this," he said, giving her the pills and wrapping the ice pack around her knee. "How does that feel?"

"Cold. Better," she sniffed.

An inexplicable surge of tenderness hit him. He placed his hand on her hair and ruffled it gently.

"What do you think?" she asked quietly.

"About your knee?"

She shook her head quietly.

"About your house?"

"It's not my house. It's my parents's house."

He debated for a moment before answering honestly.

"This place is … interesting." He hesitated for an instant, then raised his eyes so he was staring right into hers. "Maybe a bit absurd."

If she didn't see that, there wasn't much future for the two of them. And he'd be kidding himself if he didn't admit he had been imagining a future where the two of them could be together.

She stared at him for a moment, then broke out in laughter. "It is, isn't it?"

His mouth went dry. She was so beautiful. He wanted to take her upstairs and make wild, sweet, love to her.

That's not what she needs.

"Rest for a bit, Roy. Let the ice and painkillers do their work, then see how the knee feels."

15

Sierra

When she woke up next, it was dark, and she was warm. She recognized the smell of the woolen throw that usually lived over the sofa. She was drooling over something—as she opened her eyes, she prayed it wasn't Rémy's leg. But no, he was sitting by her feet, her legs elevated on his lap.

Great. I'm drooling all over the couch.

She sat up, surprised when her knee didn't immediately seize in pain.

"How's the knee, Roy?"

"Better. I don't think I damaged anything."

"It's less swollen than it was a couple hours ago."

"I've been asleep that long?"

"You were tired. How are you feeling now?"

"Good." Her stomach rumbled loudly. "Hungry."

Rémy laughed. "I went to the kitchen to make you some food, but I don't think there's anything edible in there."

"Yeah, I haven't been grocery shopping for a while. I think I have some chocolate in my room."

"Chocolate? I'm not having chocolate for dinner, Roy. We need real food."

"You're a bit of a health nut," she said affectionately. "What time is it? How about we order from Real Greens?"

His stomach rumbled in response.

"Okay, it's settled, then. Let me call them."

Half an hour later, they sat sharing a tempeh stirfry and an avocado supergreen salad.

"I don't think I've ever had this much green together ... except maybe that week I stayed at your place," she said, over a mouthful of food. "We ate a lot of green then."

"I'll have to stick around to make sure you eat your vegetables, then," he said. She saw the blush spread over his cheeks and felt the heat on hers at the same time.

Is he serious?

"So ... what's the deal with this house? How long have you lived here?"

"My parents bought this house when I was little, but we never spent much time here." She cringed inside. She wasn't about to describe their penthouse apartments in Paris and New York.

"And what's up with the art pieces? Do they have an art gallery, or something?"

"Or something. My mother discovered art a few years ago. She likes collecting pieces. My father ... he likes to make my mother happy."

He stuck a large piece of tempeh in his mouth and chewed furiously. Sierra wished she could read his mind.

"This ... does it change the way you think about me?"

"What? The fact that you live in a museum? Or the fact that your parents are rich like Croesus?"

She glared at him, then spooned some grilled avocado into her mouth. It tasted chalky, but she'd eat this every day if it meant she could eat with him.

"I'm kidding, Roy. I don't give a crap about the kind of house your parents live in."

Sierra studied him carefully. There was no deception in his tone. He was truly and coolly unimpressed by her parents's house.

"You really aren't impressed."

"I'm impressed by you. Does that count?"

"I mean, you don't care about them," she said. As someone who'd often been pursued because of the money her parents had, she needed him to say it out loud.

"The only thing I care about," he continued, "is that they treat you well."

She remembered her mother's little outburst at the hospital.

"My mother's not so bad. She's just … particular about some things."

"Like her beautiful, sexy daughter? What would she say if she knew you and I were dating?"

Her heart somersaulted inside her chest.

"Are we dating?"

"We are, as of one hour ago."

"What happened an hour ago?"

"Check your email. You're officially a certified mountain guide, Roy. Congratulations! You could work for any company in the valley, starting tomorrow."

She jumped up from the stool she was occupying and ran straight into his arms.

"Hey! Careful with your knee," he said, twirling her around. "Or we'll have to ice it again."

"Maybe you can ice it in bed," she said, wrapping her arms tighter around his wide shoulders.

He opened his mouth to reply, then closed it again quickly as his phone rang.

"Rémy," he said, picking up. "Gael, I'm here with Sierra, I'm going to put you on speaker phone."

"Hi," Sierra said shyly.

"Just wanted to let you both know that Pietro and Gina just went home with their families."

"Are they both okay?"

"It's a miracle," Gael said. "Particularly in her case."

"She was buried for over thirty minutes."

"I know. She doesn't remember much." There was

a short pause, and Sierra was sure all three of them were thinking the same thing—that it was likely better this way.

"They wanted to thank you. They both realize they never would have survived if it wasn't for you."

"They don't need to thank us," she said quickly. "I'm glad we were in the right place at the right time to be able to help."

Rémy ran his hand along her collar bone and down her arm.

"Hey," she mouthed.

"Anyway, just wanted to let you both know."

"Wait," Sierra interrupted. "How's Damien's son?"

"He's okay. His grandfather picked him up at school and brought him home. I hear they were playing Lego together by the time Damien arrived. Hold on, I have another call. Thanks again, both."

They hung up to the phone, still holding on to each other. It was as if they couldn't keep their hands off each other anymore.

"Let's go up to my bedroom," she said. "It's the only room in the house that doesn't have art work."

"You should have said so before."

Sierra whooped as Rémy picked her up.

"I can walk, you know?"

"I know. Let me carry you."

"**I**'ve waited so long for this."

Rémy twisted her nipple gently between his finger and his thumb. There was a hunger in his face, as he watched her expression, that made her think of a wild animal.

She wanted to please that wild side of him—to let him know without words that she'd do anything he wanted, that she'd endure anything, if only he kept looking at her like this.

"Look at these pretty pink nipples. So responsive. I'm going to pinch them until they go dark with need," he promised.

Despite his words, there was something cautious in his eyes as he stared into hers, and she realized he was asking for permission. She knew he would stop the moment she asked him to. Which would be a shame, because stopping was the furthest thing from her mind. Her body wanted him, had wanted him ever since their first time together—and to have him finally here, in her home, to know that they were no longer denying each other ... it was almost more than she could bear.

She pushed at his chest and twisted her body to look in the drawer of her bedside table. There, in the far back, she finally found the object she was looking for—her metallic nipple clamps. She clutched the clamps in her fist, dropping them in his larger hand.

"Don't be gentle," she whispered in his ear. She

didn't want gentle, careful sex. She wanted the two of them to rock each other's world.

His gasp was her reward when he recognized the object in his hands.

"You're going to make me come on the spot, sweetheart."

"Don't," she said bravely. "That would be a waste."

"So ... these clamps ... tell me how you use them."

Not often enough.

"Do you put them on when you're touching yourself?" he asked, undeterred by her silence. He massaged her right breast, then moved in to suck and worship the tight bud, which tightened even further under the assault.

"Take a deep breath, Sierra," he said in a deep, controlled voice.

As he tightened the little vise around her turgid nipple, she felt the breath rush out of her lungs. It hurt, and then a few seconds later it hurt even more. It hurt in such a delicious way that she was certain she'd never used the clamps right before until now.

"Beautiful." He moved to the other nipple, giving it exactly the same treatment. When he was done, he flicked the chain between them.

He raised her chin so she was looking straight into his eyes. "Say *less* if you want me to reduce the pressure, *off* if you want me to remove them, sweetheart. Otherwise, these stay on."

She nodded once, to let him know she understood, then uttered a different word.

"More."

She watched as he tightened the clamps further on her aching nubs. The sharp pleasure-meets-pain-meets-pleasure cycle was intense, and made her draw breath.

His fingers flicked at the chain between her breasts, sending waves of desire through her body. She grabbed his hand and pulled it towards her core.

"Impatient. I like it." He pushed a thick finger inside her—then a second finger joined in, scissoring inside her.

"You're burning, sweetheart. How much do you need my cock inside you?"

All she could do was whimper and shift her hips to try and get more of him inside her. More friction. More pleasure.

"When your knee is completely healed," he whispered roughly, "I'm going to place you on your knees, palms against this thick headboard, and pound into you from behind while I flick this chain."

The promise made her whimper.

"For now, stay right where you are, sweetheart. Open your legs and let me see that pretty pink pussy."

His fingers left her for an instant while he sheathed himself. The sudden, empty feeling made her want to cry.

Then he was back. His cock entered her slowly, stretching her almost to the point of pain. As her body got used to him, the slight pain eased into the deepest pleasure she'd ever felt.

Her nails scratched along his back, eliciting a ragged groan from him.

Each time he pumped inside her, he pressed against her pubic bone, the pressure at once too much and not enough.

Not nearly enough.

She slipped her index finger in his mouth and he licked greedily, as if he already knew where it was going to go afterwards. Then she slid her finger down to her clit, timing it so she stroked the little pleasure center in time with the thick cock inside her pussy.

Yes.

Yes.

Her back arched off the bed. In that instant just before she came, Rémy removed the nipple clamps. The feeling of the blood rushing back all at once took her over the edge, deep into the strongest orgasm she'd ever experienced.

Her inner muscles shook and quivered around his thick cock as he drove himself hard and fast towards his own completion.

Finally, he bared his teeth, roaring his release and collapsing on top of her, as if he no longer had the strength to hold himself up. Instead of making her feel trapped, his weight felt comforting, like a large, warm blanket.

Finally, Rémy left her, holding on to the condom carefully. He was back after a few seconds, his large body draped around hers. His hands caressed the soft weight of her breasts.

"Hey," she complained.

"Just checking to make sure I didn't hurt you."

"You didn't hurt me. That was ... I don't have the words to describe it."

"Good?"

She laughed. "Very good."

They lay together in silence for a few minutes longer. Sleep beckoned, but she was still too keyed up to sleep.

"I'm glad we're dating."

His rumbling laugh resonated against her skin. "I'm glad as well, Roy."

"We should get some sleep."

The words were barely out of her mouth when his phone rang.

"Rémy." His tone softened as he listened to the person on the other side of the phone. "Yes. No, of course. Happy to help. I'll meet you tomorrow morning. Thanks, Damien, good night."

"That was Damien." Rémy's expression was serious.

"Is his kid okay?"

"He's fine. Damien was calling about something else. I don't know if you heard about the two thieves who were targeting homes in the area since last summer?"

She nodded, her eyes wide. "They robbed one of our neighbors. Thank goodness the family wasn't home at the time. But I thought they were caught months ago?"

Rémy nodded grimly. "Apparently they escaped this morning, during the transfer to another prison."

"Shit. Well, I guess they'll be in Switzerland or Belgium by now."

"Except they hid up in the mountains around here for months before, so the police think they might try that again."

"What did Damien want?"

"His team has been tasked with coordinating the search out here in the mountains, and they're looking for some ice climbers to support."

Her blood froze in her veins at his words. "You'll be careful, right, Rémy?"

"Always. You know that. Damien doesn't think we'll find anything out there, anyway. Come here," he said, bringing her onto his shoulder. "Let's get some sleep, so we can get tired again."

16

Rémy

W*hat a wasted day.*

Rémy turned the shower in his apartment as hot it would go, hoping to get rid of the cold that had seeped into his bones over the course of the day—a day spent out in the mountains, babysitting a group of Paris policemen who couldn't find an ice axe if it was staring them in the face.

Their little group hadn't found any sign of the fugitives, and the Paris inspector leading the search was more and more convinced the men had left the country by now and gone back to their native Slovenia.

Still shivering, Rémy dressed in a pair of dark blue

jeans and an olive henley before heading back out the door again and into his car.

He was almost at Sierra's gate—which seemed larger even than it had the previous day—before realizing he hadn't called to tell her he was coming.

Too late now.

He rang the doorbell and waited patiently.

Give her time, she's got to make it across that huge house.

"Hello?" she asked cautiously.

"Hi, Roy."

"Rémy!"

He drove inside and parked on the same spot as the night before, opened the passenger door and brought out the box he'd stopped for on his way over. "Organic, whole-grain, veggie—"

"Pizza?" she interrupted, eagerly ripping the box from his hands. "Why didn't you say so before?"

He laughed. "I'm learning the way to your heart, Roy."

Her eyes grew serious. "You're already in my heart, Rémy. I've been worried about you all day. How was it?"

"Uneventful. Cold. I think the city police are starting to understand the impossibility of dividing Mont Blanc into search quadrants."

"Come inside," she said, ushering him ahead of her.

He took his jacket off and placed it on a hook near

the door. "Brrr ... it's almost as cold in here as it is outside. Was it this cold last night? You should come to my place tomorrow if your parents can't afford to heat the house."

Sierra laughed. "You get used to it. A stable, cool temperature is best for the artwork."

"Okay, we're definitely going to my place tomorrow."

"I can turn the fireplace on, though. That should help."

"Never mind. We'll be warm enough once we get in bed," he said, smiling.

"But first, I'm having a slice of this delicious-smelling pizza. Hmmm," she moaned, peering into the box.

The sounds she made went straight to his cock.

"You know, I didn't take you for a pizza lover."

"This pizza is different. Wait till you—"

"You had me at pizza, Rémy," she laughed, turning the oven on. She poured some water for him and a beer for herself, and together they sat around the steel island to wait for the timer.

"How's your knee, Roy? Did you call Dr. Daniels?"

She stretched a shapely leg. "I don't think I need to... I did all my stretching exercises, and it's feeling okay."

"It looks pretty okay, too," he said, reaching down to caress her knee. She didn't move away, even parted her legs to allow him better access.

"Tsk, tsk, that's not the way to ensure you get pizza, you know?"

She closed her legs quickly. "Believe me, we're not going anywhere until I've eaten."

The oven dinged and Sierra put the pizza onto a large serving plate.

He watched her take a large bite. "So. What do you think?"

"Hmm ... it *is* delicious. But I would still choose pepperoni anytime over these ... what are these little things?"

"Artichokes, Roy. Artichokes."

"It's really good pizza. Thank you, Rémy."

"What are you going to do now?" he asked, watching her take a large bite.

She didn't pretend to misunderstand his question. "I updated my CV today and sent out a few copies already. One of them went to your employer."

"I'll call Laetitia and let her know. She'll move you to the top of the pile."

"Is she the CEO?"

"More important. She's the administrative assistant." He smiled gently. "Any guide company would be lucky to have you, Roy."

"Thank you. It means a lot to hear you say that." She took another large bite, almost done with her first slice. "You know, these artichokes are growing on me." She paused for a second. "I also started looking for apartments. I found a couple of places already."

He drained his glass of water before replying. "You did?"

"One is right in the center of town. A small studio—third floor walk-up, with a brilliant view of the mountains beyond. Another one is up in Les Plans. That one has a lot of light, and even a tiny garden."

"So not in Les Houches?"

"God, no. I want to get as far away from here as possible. I'm going to visit both of them tomorrow."

It was on the tip of his tongue to ask her to move in with him, but he stopped himself just in time. She sounded so excited about getting her own place, and the last thing he wanted to do was scare her off. Although he'd been thinking about her for months, it was only yesterday that they'd officially started dating. He wasn't about to risk that.

"Are you okay, Rémy? You look worried, suddenly."

"I'm fine. Just thinking about tomorrow."

"Do you have to go back to the search?"

"No. I have a client tomorrow. A family with three kids, out for a day of light skiing. Should be relaxing."

"Relaxing is good." She patted her stomach. "I'm stuffed. How about we relax together on the couch?"

Rémy followed her to the living area. They hadn't spent long enough together for him to tell her what he was thinking—that he would like to spend each and every night with her.

Waves lapped at the side of the boat, creating a gentle, rocking motion. One, a bit larger than the others, shook the boat from side to side. Looking overboard, she waited for the rocking to subside. As she stared, the sea receded, and soon the boat was lying on the sand, still rocking. The absurdity of the situation hit her then, and she opened her eyes to find Rémy shaking her arm lightly.

You were dreaming.

His hands went to his lips in the universal sign for silence.

He leaned close to her ear. "Are you expecting anyone? I heard a sound downstairs," he said in a low voice.

Sierra shook her head quickly. She'd spoken to her parents earlier, and they were both in New York. And Rosa wouldn't come to the house in the middle of the night.

Rémy's body tensed against her—he must have ears like a mountain lion—and then she heard it too.

Crack. Crack.

"Stay here and lock yourself inside this room," he said. He was already shucking on his jeans and boots. He didn't bother with the socks, but picked up a sweatshirt on his way out the door.

She put a hand to his arm to stop him. Something told her they'd be safer together.

"I'm coming with you," she whispered. From the chair next to the bed she picked up a pair of black leggings, trainers and a sweatshirt, putting everything on over her nightshirt.

Rémy placed her phone in her hand. His gray eyes were as serious as she'd ever seen them. "Be ready to dial 112."

Together, they made their way downstairs. The living room was dark—the only light came from the moonlight making its way through the bay windows. The front door was closed, and so were all the windows.

"There's nobody here," she said, relieved.

Sierra found herself relaxing for the first time since she'd woken up.

Rémy's expression was still tense. He pointed downstairs with his finger. It was clear he wanted to search the whole house.

This second staircase wasn't wide enough for the two of them to take side-by-side. Rémy took the lead and Sierra followed him down the stairs. At the bottom, she reached over to stand beside him—and stared out at the balcony door.

It was ajar.

Tension coiled up her spine.

"I didn't leave it like that," she whispered.

Frigid mountain air slipped into the house through the gap.

What else could have slipped through?

"Let's get out of here, Sierra."

She looked down at her trainers. "But I'm not wearing ..."

He pointed to the ski room, still speaking in a soft, low voice. "Grab your coat and a pair of hiking boots. We need to—"

And then a man walked out from the laundry room, calm as anything. He was tall and broad, dressed in some kind of dark blue uniform. His huge pot belly bulged, spreading below the jacket.

Those are not his clothes.

Sierra looked up at the dark object in his hand, and her fear ratcheted higher, as if somebody had turned a crank in her mind. Suddenly, it was hard to breathe. She'd never seen a gun in person before. It would have terrified her anywhere. But to see it in her own house ... Her body shook like a reed in the wind.

Make the call.

Sierra tightened her finger on her phone.

"Press that button and I'll shoot off your hand," the man growled. Her finger stopped in mid-air. "Good. Now drop the phone. Kick it towards me."

Heart racing, Sierra did as the man asked. When she looked up again, Rémy had taken a step forward, so he now stood between her and the man. As the man turned towards him, Rémy lifted his hands and sprayed something at the man's face.

The man roared and covered his eyes.

Rémy grabbed her hand, pulling at her. "Run, Sierra!"

"Stop!" the man shouted, but Sierra didn't stop. She squeezed in through the door and out to the lawn beyond. Her trainers slipped on an icy patch but she recovered her balance and kept going, skirting around the pool.

A shot rang out, the sound deafening in the silence of the night.

Behind her, Rémy grunted.

Has he been hit?

No!

"Keep going!" Rémy shouted, his footsteps right behind hers.

She concentrated on putting one foot of another, looking for the tree-line at the edge of her parents's property. The further they moved from the house, the harder it was to see where they were going. To make matters worse, her trainers were completely inadequate for the terrain. She slipped onto the snow but picked herself up again quickly, her leggings now soaked with rain.

We'll freeze out here.

"We're not going to freeze out here."

She hadn't realized she'd said it out loud.

Rémy placed a steadying hand on her arm. He kept his voice low. "Slow down, Sierra. I think we lost them."

"Them? I only saw one."

"He was calling out for somebody else. I think I know who they are."

The too-small uniform finally registered. The man had been wearing somebody else's clothes.

Her mouth fell open, but no sound came out. She felt as if she'd suddenly entered another dimension. This couldn't be happening to them. Not here. Not now.

She watched, uncomprehending, as Rémy took off his black sweatshirt. It was only once he approached her with it that she understood he intended to bundle her inside. It was warm and smelled like him. Tears popped in her eyes, and all the blinking in the world wasn't going to hold them back.

"No," she whispered.

"Shh, I'm okay. I'm never cold."

She stopped arguing as she noticed a dark stain on the sleeve. She touched it—it wasn't just a stain, it was a hole, matched by the blood dripping down his arm. The first drops fell onto the snow.

"Shit," he said.

"You're bleeding."

"It's just a scratch," he said.

"Really? Can you be more cliché?" She tore a strap from the bottom of her T-shirt and tied it tightly around his upper arm.

"Thanks."

Rémy brought something out of his jeans pocket. Sierra had never been so thankful to see a phone before. He covered the screen's glow with his hand as he dialed.

"Gael. I'm at Sierra's place." Rémy looked at her

inquiringly and she rattled off the address. "Two men broke in. Yes. I think it's them. We've managed to lose them in the yard but—"

A loud crack made Rémy shut down the call. Then another. These men were not trained in stealth.

"We need to keep going," Sierra said, tugging on Rémy's arm.

"That's what they'll expect us to do," he said in a low voice." We need to double back towards the house."

He led the way, keeping low, and she did the same, until they reached the spot they'd left just minutes earlier. The patio door was still open.

"What do we do now?" she asked. It felt incredibly exposed out here. If the men turned back towards the house, they would see them immediately.

"We climb," Rémy said. "Gael and his team will be here soon."

Sierra thought for a moment. It'd be cold as hell, but it was a good idea. There was no way those men would expect them to go up.

They started climbing side by side. It was hard going, in trainers and soaked-through leggings, but Rémy was with her every step of the way until they reached the main floor of the house, which was covered in vines.

"Use them," Rémy cautioned, "but don't put too much weight on any of them."

Up and up they climbed. Soon Sierra's fingers were so cold, they felt less like fingers and more like claws. Each time she wanted to move upwards, she had to force herself to unclench them from their current hold.

Beside her, Rémy seemed to be having no such trouble, even though he was in a T-shirt and boots. When they got out of this, she was going to—

Clang.

Shit.

She'd grabbed on to a pipe that had a vine hidden behind it.

They both stood very still. Sierra held her breath until he lungs felt like they would explode.

Please, don't let them hear us—

The rumbling and sloshing coming from the yard quickly dispelled such hope.

They're coming for us.

Sierra froze, turning to Rémy. If they were going to be shot as they stuck to the wall, she wanted his face to be the last thing she saw—except he wasn't there anymore. He'd moved down below her. She felt his hand press on her leg, pushing her upwards.

"Keep going, Sierra. Get out." he whispered.

Then he was gone.

He jumped.

He left me.

Rémy landed on the terrace below and rolled, making quite the racket.

Sierra stuck to the wall, petrified. She couldn't keep going without him. She pressed her lips tightly to stop herself from whimpering.

He's giving me a chance to escape.

Finally, she forced her frozen fingers to unclench from their current hold and shifted quietly upwards. She had to get to the upstairs balcony, and out of sight.

Rémy

Rémy landed on the cold, hard ground, glad for the snow that somewhat helped break his fall.

He rolled to his knees, making zero effort at stealth—the more noise he made, the more likely it'd be that Sierra's movements would go undetected.

A kick to the ribs sent him back to the ground.

"Who the fuck are you?" It was the man who'd shot at them earlier. He man spoke English with an Eastern European accent.

"I just came to feed the cat," Rémy said.

A second, younger man roared with mirthless laughter. "In the middle of the night? We saw the girl. Where is she now?"

"She ran. I lost sight of her in the woods."

"He's lying. She's going to call the police, she's going to—"

"Let me ask again," the first man said, ignoring his companion. He grabbed on to Rémy's pony tail, pulling upwards. "Where is the woman?"

Rémy allowed himself to be pulled up to his knees. He wanted to be on his feet anyway. If these men were stupid enough to help him get there—

A noise sounded above them.

Sierra.

No.

Rémy pulled up his elbow and rammed it into the belly of the man behind him. As expected, the man's hold on his hair loosened, and Rémy took the chance to jump up and turn, punching him in the nose. There was a satisfying crunch, and blood spurted onto the pristine white snow.

Fear exploded in bright colors inside Rémy. He wasn't a fighter, but he knew he had to fight, or he and Sierra wouldn't survive the night. As the man howled and clutched the ruined appendage, Rémy slammed his elbow down onto the back of the man's head, watching with relief as the large man fell, unconscious, to the ground.

The second man.

Find the second—

A short rang out in the night. Rémy instinctively covered his head with his arms, but the man wasn't aiming at him. He'd figured out where Sierra was, and he was aiming at the wall Sierra was climbing.

Rémy didn't know enough about full-contact fighting to disarm the man safely—but he wasn't about to let him shoot again.

An idea came to him then, and he launched himself at the man, pulling both of them sideways until, together, they fell onto the frozen pool.

The thin layer of ice held for an instant. Rémy cursed loudly—he' been counting on the fact the ice wouldn't be thick enough to withstand the weight of two grown men.

He pulled the man firmly against his body and rolled them both towards the center of the pool, listening for the popping and crackling that told him the ice was about to crack.

Rémy took a deep breath, just as the ice broke through and they both fell into the dark water. The intense freezing sensation engulfed him, but Rémy was mentally prepared, and used to dealing with cold —the man sputtering and thrashing in his arms, not so much.

Rémy slammed the man's arm against the edge of the ice. Once, twice, three times, until the thick fingers opened up and the gun fell out of his hand. Rémy felt it sink to the bottom of the pool.

The man sobbed. Again and again he grabbed onto the ice, but each piece he grabbed broke under his weight, and each time his movements were weaker.

"Help ..." he gasped through blue, trembling lips.

Moving just out of the man's reach, Rémy treaded

water and took a couple of deep, slow breaths—enough to convince his body not to go into shock. Though the cold *could* kill a man, given enough time, Rémy knew he had enough time to get to shelter, as long as he remained calm.

He eyed the struggling man dispassionately and forced himself to swim away from him, towards the far edge of the pool.

His boots seemed to weigh a ton, but at least he was only wearing a T-shirt on top. Had he been wearing his winter jacket, he knew his arms would have felt impossibly heavy. He reached the edge and pulled himself up on shaky arms, rolling his body onto the snow, nimble like an elephant seal.

Just need to rest for an instant.

He lay there, his cheek against the ground, vaguely surprised that the snow under his face felt warm.

That's not a good sign.

Get the hell up, Rémy.

It was a noise from the other side of the pool that had him pushing himself onto his hands and knees. The freezing outside air pummeled his body, but he pushed himself until he was standing upright.

Through blurry eyes, he saw the man in the pool. He'd managed to reach the edge and was kicking weakly, barely managing to keep his head out of water.

Before Rémy could decide whether or not to help him, he realized the man he'd thought he'd knocked out was gone. Then he saw the bloody hand print against the open patio door.

He's in the house.

A cold shudder filled him that had nothing to do with the icy swim.

He'd sent Sierra into the house.

With a ragged groan, Rémy finally forced his frozen limbs to move.

Sierra

As the shot rang out, Sierra squeezed her eyes shut and pressed herself against the wall, as if that would somehow make her less of a target.

The shot pinged on the stone at least six feet away from her.

He's shooting blind.

She stuck to the wall like a limpet, wondering if the next shot would be the one to hit her, but the next shot never happened.

Instead, she heard something that sounded like a fist slamming against a side of beef, except she knew it was Rémy down there, fighting for their lives. The sound elicited a visceral reaction in her, and she had to consciously stop herself from heaving.

And even though she knew she was high up enough that she might get hurt, a part of her wanted to jump off the wall anyway. The other, more analytical part of her brain, stopped her from doing that. She wouldn't do Rémy any good if she jumped off the wall right now. She had to stick to the plan.

Reach the balcony.

Get into the house.

Open the door and the gate.

Hide and wait for the cavalry.

The first three were essential. The last one, in her mind, was optional. She wasn't about to sit and wait if Rémy was in danger.

She grappled onwards and upwards, her hands now so frozen it was hard to get them to obey, and finally reached the balcony.

Praying it would hold her weight, she transfered to the edge of the balcony and pulled herself up, no longer worried about stealth, knowing she had to get inside as quickly as possible.

Sierra crouched in front of the glass door. On the other side, her parents's large bedroom lay shrouded in darkness.

Shit.

Now what?

She didn't have anything to crack open the glass with. Then she felt in the pocket of Rémy's sweatshirt—felt the outline of a large key chain. She brought it out, grateful for the moonlight.

There was the bear repellent spray—that must be

what he'd sprayed the man with downstairs, when they'd escaped, and a second attachment that looked like a miniature emergency tool, the kind people carried to help them escape in case of a car accident.

Yes.

A little voice inside her told her these were meant for car windows, not for double-glazed panes, but she ignored that voice.

It will work.

Having never tried to break a window before, Sierra had no idea how much pressure she should use. She pressed it against the glass then pressed harder when nothing happened.

Shit.

It's not working.

A quick look at the hammer revealed a white object on the front. Almost giggling now, she removed the lid, staring at the sharp, metallic point that was revealed.

Better.

She aimed at the middle of the window and hammered once. Then again. A spider crack appeared, urging her on. The crack widened, as if in slow motion, and soon she was through the first pane.

Yes.

She aimed for the broken spot and slammed the hammer again and again. Then the hammer slipped. Her frozen fingers slammed against the broken pane, the pain brutal enough to make her scream out loud. Blood poured from her hand onto the white ground.

She clamped her lips together to make the sound stop and shifted the hammer to her other hand, stopping only to wrap the sweatshirt around her hand before she continued to hit the window, visualizing the moment when the pane would crack and her hand would go through.

Finally, it happened. She used the hammer to widen the hole until she could reach inside to unlatch it.

I just broke into my house.

She ran inside, her wet trainers squelching on the soft, light carpet. Blood dripped from her fingers, dying it pink. A deep gash bisected her palm in the joint area, where her pinky and ring fingers met. She gasped at the pain radiating from her hand.

She picked one of her mother's silk scarves where it lay on a hook by the door and wrapped it tightly around her hand, then raced out of the room and down the stairs. She hit the open button for the front gate and opened the front door, hoping against hope to see police cars behind—to see anyone—there, but the night beyond was completely dark.

Sierra held on to the door frame for support. Disappointment weighed like a heavy stone inside her, but she fought against it.

Rémy's car was there, and his keys were in the pocket. She knew Rémy would want her to drive away, but she also knew she couldn't leave him here alone.

The sounds of fighting had stopped, which could only mean one of two things.

Leaving the front door propped open, she turned to the guest coat closet and picked up one of the golf clubs her father always kept in there. She hefted the thick, substantial weight in her left hand, since the joints in her right hand refused to bend.

Thanks, Dad.

Her soaked trainers squelched with every step she took, so she took them off and continued on bare feet. At the bottom of the staircase she found herself frozen in place. It was hard to find the courage to step into the lounge.

Then a man stumbled into the house—large and barrel-shaped.

Not Rémy.

He was looking down, his hands clutching at his nose, so at first he didn't see her. She stood very still, willing him to walk by, even though her heart was hammering inside her chest.

He was so close to turning his back on her, so close to walking right by, until something—maybe her throbbing heartbeat—made him look up at the very last instant. He roared, releasing his nose, and started running across the lounge towards her. The glass flooring vibrated with each step he took.

Through her panic, a sudden idea struck her. She hit the switch on the wall beside her and held her breath. The indoor pool hidden under the lounge floor had been the largest extravagance in the very extravagant renovation her parents had carried out just a couple of years earlier. At the press of a button, the floor panels slid out, revealing a pool whose water had always been too warm for Sierra to enjoy.

She had no idea if the floor would slide out with a man's weight on it. Maybe there were sensors to stop —but no, the panels *were* sliding.

Yes.

The man danced around in a struggle to keep his balance, clearly not understanding what was going on or which way the panels were shifting. Then he seemed to understand what was happening and started racing sideways, looking to clear the edge of the pool.

Shit.

He's not going to fall in.

Sierra ran as well, keeping to the other side of the pool. She had to get outside and help Rémy.

She was almost at the patio doors, close enough that she could feel the chill coming in from outside, when the man caught up with her. He pulled on her hair—hard enough to jerk her entire body back.

How did he get here so quickly?

Losing her balance, she dropped her golf club and fell back against the man's hard body.

No.

"Stop right there. Where's the safe?"

Sierra struggled in an ocean of panic.

The safe? What safe?

"Let me go!"

In response, he pulled harder on her hair, eliciting a pained whimper from her.

"You and your boyfriend think you can fuck with us?" he snarled.

A kick to the back of her legs sent her to her knees. Sierra put out her hands to break her fall, almost fainting when her injured hand smacked the floor.

Black dots filled her vision and she clenched her teeth together to stop herself from screaming.

The man pushed her to the ground, wrenching her hands above her head. His weight on her back felt suffocating at first, and quickly became unbearable when he reached forward, his warm, fetid breath reaching into her ear.

"You don't know the things we've done," he whispered wetly. His tongue reached out to lick Sierra's ear in an obscene parody of a lover's embrace.

Bile rose from the back of her throat. She turned her head, searching desperately for the golf club. If she could just reach it—

But the golf club was gone.

The man's large hands tightened on her neck. Sierra gasped and struggled, but there was nothing she could do.

She closed her eyes. Her mind filled with thoughts of Rémy. She'd let him down. Even if it might be too late for her, she hoped the police arrived in time to help him.

Whoosh.

Crack.

The man's weight fell from her back and Sierra

could breathe again. She scrambled backwards on her butt, scuttling away from her attacker, who now lay unconscious on the ground.

Rémy stood above then, holding the club like a baseball bat. His lips were tinged blue and he seemed to have trouble coordinating his movements. He struggled to a kneeling position next to the unconscious man, using the man's own belt to tie his hands together.

Only then did his gray eyes focus on her.

"Sierra," he muttered. "Did he hurt you?"

She shook her head, then stopped as the pain in her neck intensified.

I'm alive.

Her voice, when she tried to tell him she was okay, came out as a raw whisper.

Rémy went down heavily beside her. His hands and clothes were cold against her body as he pulled her against him, but she burrowed into the cold, needing to be closer to him. The last thing she felt, before the world faded into darkness, was the sound of his steady, beating heart.

19

Rémy

He held Sierra's body to him. His fingers were too cold to feel her pulse, but he could see regular little puffs of breath leaving her body.

She's alive.

Unable to help himself, he grazed her cheek with his fingers, then pulled back when he saw how warm her skin felt, and how cold his own was in contrast.

Anger burst through him at the sight of the finger marks on Sierra's neck. He knew the kind of pressure it would take to get marks like that on another human being—the man had tried to crush Sierra's wind pipe.

Rémy, who'd never considered himself a violent man, wished he'd hit the man even harder.

He forced himself to concentrate on Sierra. That

was the only important thing at the moment—making sure she was safe, and keeping her as comfortable as possible until help arrived.

There were blood spatters on the sweatshirt, but all the blood seemed to come from her hand. Rémy carefully unwrapped the bloody scarf she'd tied around her hand, wincing at the ugly cut on her hand and fingers.

That's how the cavalry found him when they arrived, holding on to Sierra's body for dear life.

Three men ran past him. Rémy recognized the inspector leading the manhunt. Inspector Druet. He figured he should warn them that there was a man in the pool, but was having trouble getting his mouth to work.

Gael and Jens kneeled beside him.

"Are you okay, Rémy?" Gael asked.

"He tried to choke her. Her hand ..."

"I've got her. Let me take care of her," Jens said softly, pushing him gently away. Though he was too weak to stand, Rémy forced himself to scuttle aside, knowing he could trust the doctor to take care of Sierra.

"Did you decide to go for a swim?" Gael asked. His friend pulled hard on Rémy's T-shirt, and it took Rémy a moment to understand he was trying to take it off.

"Shit. Did you get shot?"

Moments later, Rémy found himself draped in Gael's warm coat. It was tight around the shoulders, but probably the warmest thing he'd ever felt in his life.

"Let me get your jeans off. I'm sure we can find—"

"No. I need to stay here with Sierra." Jens had already started an IV line and was pumping something into her.

A man Rémy had never seen before took off the belt Rémy had used and put handcuffs on the unconscious man.

"Is he the one who hurt her?" he asked, pointing at Sierra's neck.

Rémy nodded. Bitter bile rose to his throat at the memory. He'd never been as afraid before in his life as when he'd walked inside to find the man on top of Sierra, and her, lying so still. For a moment, he'd thought he was too late. If he'd been just a few seconds later—

"It's okay, Rémy. She's going to be okay," Gael said, distracting him from his thoughts.

"There's another man in the pool," Rémy finally managed.

"Damien, Drake, and Inspector Druet are on it," Gael said.

Moments later, Drake walked back inside, his expression grim, his sleeves soaked up past his elbows.

"The man didn't make it."

Rémy inhaled sharply. This was on him. He could have saved the man's life, but he'd made the decision to leave him in the pool while he went inside to check on Sierra. In doing so, he'd effectively killed the man.

A man who was trying to kill you.

If you'd stopped to save him, you might not have been in time to save Sierra.

It was a decision he was happy to live with.

"We need to ask you some questions," Inspector Druet said. The tall, somber man from the day before looked like he'd just won the lottery.

Out of the corner of his eye, Rémy saw Sierra geting loaded onto a stretcher.

"I need to go to the hospital with her," he stated.

"Not until you've answered—"

"He's hypothermic," Jens announced, coming up behind him with a thermometer. "Let's get him to the hospital first, and you can speak to him once we've gotten his core temperature up."

Inspector Druet nodded quickly. If he was irritated, he didn't let on.

Rémy threw Jens a grateful look, and followed Sierra to the waiting ambulance.

20

Sierra

A pair of hands reached out behind her on the couch and fluffed her pillows.

Sierra turned her head to look at Rémy, who'd been behaving like a mother hen ever since they were both released from the hospital.

They'd gone back to his place, where she'd slept for most of the day.

She wasn't worried about her parents's house. Rémy's friend, Gael, had stayed behind and waited for Rosa to arrive. He'd also, she knew from speaking to Rosa, cleaned up most of the mess and blood off the floor and arranged to get the broken window fixed. Sierra was grateful. Rosa hadn't deserved to see that.

Sierra would have to thank the man next time she saw him.

"He's not saying anything," Rémy said quietly, stepping out so she no longer had to crane her neck to look at him.

Sierra gave him a questioning look.

"The surviving fugitive. He hasn't said a single word yet. Inspector Druet's like a dog with a bone, though. This time, he's escorting the man back to Paris himself, where he will await his trial." Rémy paused for a second. A shadow crossed his eyes. "The inspector thinks it's possible they saw me at the search party and followed me home afterwards, and from there to your place. Maybe I brought them to you." The anguish in his expression hurt more than her neck.

She shook her head, careful not to wince. Thankfully, her voice box and windpipe hadn't been damaged, but it was still difficult to talk and swallow. She knew how lucky she'd been, though. She looked down at her bandaged hand. Though the cut had been deep, and required twelve stitches to close it, the doctors had found no sign of nerve damage and expected her to make a full recovery.

Rémy had been lucky as well, since the bullet had gone clean through his arm without doing too much damage.

"That doesn't make sense," she said, speaking quietly so as not to strain her voice and worry Rémy further. "He couldn't know you'd be heading over to my place. And he asked me where the safe was. I think the house must have been on their target list before they were captured, and they figured it'd be empty. It was bad luck. Or good luck, if you think about it, since we stopped them from hurting anyone else."

"How can you be so—"

She reached out for him and brought him down on the couch next to her.

"Rémy, stop, please. We're together. Back in that house, when—" She stopped herself, not wanting Rémy to visualize the scene. "When I didn't know if we would be okay or not, all I wanted was a chance for us to be together."

Rémy looked at her, a questioning, hopeful expression on his face.

Time to put myself out there.

"We have that chance now. I want you."

There.

It's definitely out there.

"I want you too," he said. "But I—"

She pulled herself up straighter and kissed through his objection. She was done with objections.

"Hey," he grumbled. "You didn't let me finish."

"I know what you were going to say. And I don't need for us to take it slow."

He smiled wryly. "What if I was just going to say *I* need to take it slow?"

"Then I'd call you out as a liar," Sierra replied,

straddling him and running her left hand along the outline of his thick, hard cock.

He groaned, his hips flexing reflexively against her, then stilled her hand with his larger one.

"Stay with me, Sierra." His Adam's apple bobbed up and down. "Not just tonight. Cancel those apartment visits. Move in with me."

She looked into Rémy's deep gray eyes. "If you're saying this because—"

"No," he said, decisively. His hand held on to hers now, moving her away from his cock. "I wanted to say this to you when you first brought up the apartment search, but you were so excited about it and I didn't want to spoil that for you."

"What's changed now?"

"I almost lost you last night. I don't want to wait another minute for our life together to start." He went on in a rush. "I love you, Sierra."

"I love you too, Rémy. So much." Tears filled her eyes. At his horrified expression, she laughed and tried to blink them away. "Ignore me. They're happy tears."

Rémy kissed her, then. "I'm never going to ignore anything about you, Roy."

"You do know my mother will probably want to visit, right?"

"She's very welcome to visit, as long as she doesn't try to convince you that we should move into their monstrous place instead."

"You really didn't like the house, huh," she laughed.

He shrugged. "I admit I hated the place from the moment I saw the giant terracotta warrior in the entry hallway."

Sierra smothered a laugh. "Don't tell my mother that. She loves that thing."

"I won't tell her, then. I want her to like me, Sierra. I want both your parents to like me, because I know they're important to you. But I don't want anything from them. You and I—we're making our own life together."

Sierra wondered how she could have gotten so lucky.

She held on as Rémy stood up, lifting her with him and wrapping her legs around his hips. The contact was strong and pleasurable, and if he'd only taken her jeans off first—

"None of that, Sierra. I'm just taking you to bed. You need to rest—"

She shifted herself closer to his erection.

"None of what?" she asked innocently, then laughed at the strained expression on his face. "Take me to bed, Rémy."

-- -- -- -- -- -- --

Read on for a preview of Mountain Struggle,
Mont Blanc Rescue Book 1...

175

PREVIEW: MONT BLANC RESCUE
BOOK 1

Damien

Damien Gray stood up, stretching to relieve the kinks in his neck and shoulders. He wasn't sleeping well these days, and sitting at his desk most of the day hadn't helped.

He wondered if he should be upgrading his bed to a Super King—in recent months Jamie, his six-year-old son, had made a habit of wandering into Damien's bed sometime between three and four in the morning. The boy was typically fast asleep minutes later, but by then it was too late for Damien—he was fully awake.

He often spent an hour lying beside his son, watching his little chest rise and fall gently, before giving up and getting out of bed. Asleep, Jamie seemed younger than his six years, and Damien was often returned in his mind to the moment four years earlier when the boy's mother had turned up on Damien's doorstep with the toddler in tow.

Damien looked down at his watch—almost five p.m., and he still had to stop by the store on his way home. He and Jamie were going to teach Tess, Jamie's nanny, how to cook chicken fajitas.

As always when he thought of Tess, he felt a completely inappropriate surge of desire course through him.

Stay away.

She's twenty-five years old, and she's great with Jamie.

Don't fuck it up.

Damien turned off his computer and lined up the papers on his desk. He'd have to come in early tomorrow to wrap up a couple of reports, but it was worth it to spend the evening with his son.

His hand was already on the door handle when his cell phone rang.

"Gray," he answered, forcing himself to tone down his impatience.

"*Commandant?*" The word was spoken in a lilting Canadian accent.

Damien and Drake Jacobs, his second-in-command at the Chamonix *Peloton de Gendarmerie de Haute Montagne*—PGHM for short—had worked together long enough that, as soon as he heard the other man's somber tone, Damien knew his dinner plans would have to be put on hold.

"We just got a call from Cosmiques. Two climbers went out on a climb early this morning, they were expecting them back for a late lunch, but they haven't arrived yet."

"Where are you now?"

"In the car, on my way to the office."

"Can you pick me up?"

"Sure thing, I'll be there in three minutes, *Commandant*."

There was a time when getting ready would have involved little more for Damien than grabbing his uniform jacket and the pack he kept ready, but that was before he had a son.

He sat down behind his desk again, feeling every one of his thirty-six years, and sighed softly before picking up the phone. It rang three times before anybody picked up on the other end.

"Hello?"

"Tess? It's Damien. Is Jamie there with you?"

She sounded slightly out of breath. "He's under the couch. I'm under the kitchen table. We're playing at being whales."

Damien smiled despite himself. His son's imagination never ceased to amaze him—it was definitely not something the boy had inherited from him.

"Should I put him on?" she continued in her soft Oxfordshire accent.

"No, please don't." He and Jamie didn't communicate well on the phone, perhaps because their only phone interactions happened whenever Damien was cancelling plans on his son—something that happened altogether too frequently. "Something came up ... I'm not going to make it to dinner."

There was a moment of silence. Tess knew how much tonight's dinner meant to Jamie.

"I'm sorry," he continued. "I need to go up to the Aiguille du Midi station. I don't know what time I'll be home. Please tell Jamie—"

"It's okay, you don't have to explain," she interrupted quietly. Then, in a louder voice, "Jamie and I were thinking of visiting John. He might make us raclette for dinner."

"Raclette!" cried out a little voice. "Papaw's going to make raclette for us!"

"Yes! Let me call him and find out if he's home," Tess said. She was still holding the phone to her ear, but clearly wasn't speaking to Damien anymore.

Something swelled in Damien's chest. Tess had done it again—managed to distract Jamie so the boy wouldn't realize that Damien had let him down again. A part of him knew this wouldn't last—soon Jamie would be too old to be so easily tricked. But not today.

"Thank you," he breathed.

"We'll be here when you get back," she said. "Stay safe."

Damien's phone pinged with a message from Drake.

Be there in two minutes.

Damien put on his tactical jacket and changed into his boots, making sure the liners of his tactical pants were inside the boots. Even in the middle of summer it got cold up in the mountains.

He sent his father a quick message, letting him know Tess was going to call him. He wrote in English. Though Damien was born and had always lived in France, his American father had always spoken with him in English, and Damien was equally comfortable in both languages. It sometimes seemed to Damien that, forty years after moving to Chamonix, his father still spoke French like he'd only just arrived.

Though he and his father were very different and had grown apart since Damien's mother's death, Damien knew he could always count on his father where Jamie was concerned. Most importantly, should something happen to him, he knew John would take good care of Jamie. It was the reason he could do what he did, as a single father—otherwise, the risk would have been too great.

He pressed send on the message and put the phone back in his pocket, his attention now focused on the missing climbers.

The mountain hut's manager shrugged. "Normally we wouldn't even have noticed they were missing until nighttime, but Mr. Reeds was very particular about lunch being served for them at two p.m. in the upstairs terrace."

"Do you know why that is?" Damien asked. The

Refuge des Cosmiques was incredibly popular with mountaineers and skiers, but wasn't known for providing special service to anyone.

The manager looked at him impatiently. "Yes, of course I know. He's going to ask *Mademoiselle* Lefevre to marry him as soon as they're back from their climb. He's planned a lovely proposal."

And no doubt given you a nice tip for your troubles.

"And you're sure they went to La Rébuffat?"

"Of course I'm sure," the manager huffed. "The two of them spoke of nothing else last night. The lady's climbed it several times before."

Damien looked down at his notes.

"So Mademoiselle Lefevre is a strong climber."

"Stronger than him, for sure. Poor Mr. Reeds was a wreck last night thinking about it. He said it was his first multi-pitch climb."

"And they went out alone?"

The manager nodded. "They left at four-thirty this morning."

A muscle ticked behind Drake's jaw, and Damien knew his friend was thinking the same thing he was.

Those two shouldn't have been anywhere near La Rébuffat—at least not on their own.

"Thank you for your help, *Monsieur* Lagarde."

"Jacques. Please call me Jacques. Let me know if we can help in any way."

Damien and Drake turned around and walked to the helicopter, where Lieutenant Kat Barreau, their pilot, waited for them. Beside her stood two lean, strong men, one of them dark-haired, the other one with hair so blond it was almost white.

"Gael," said Damien, addressing the tan, dark-haired man. "What are you doing here? I thought you were off today."

Gael turned and looked up at them. At five-eleven, he was a few inches shorter than Damien and Drake. His dark green eyes crinkled at the corners when he smiled, pointing towards the climbing packs on the ground next to them.

"This is what I do in my time off, *jefe*. Rémy and I were climbing nearby, so we came over to help." Gael León was their team's most experienced climber.

Damien nodded his head at Rémy, a mountain guide and avalanche forecaster from St. Gervais who often volunteered with the PGHM. Damien knew Gael and Rémy often went out to conquer impossible climbs together.

"How's my favorite NATO team doing?" Rémy asked, flashing very white teeth.

"Don't call us that," Gael asked, sighing dramatically.

Damien laughed. Rémy was referring to the multiple nationalities that made up Damien's team. Only he and Kat had been born in France, and in Damien's case he was only half French. The rest of the team had come to Chamonix from elsewhere. They all spoke at least decent French—you couldn't become a member of the PGHM without it—but each had excelled in other areas of their training.

Drake Jacobs, his Canadian second-in-command, was bilingual, of course. He was also one of the strongest men Damien had ever met—both physically and mentally. Hiro Habu, the son of a famous Japanese model and a French businessman who had come to France in his early teens, was the best dog handler Damien had ever encountered. Gael, a world-famous climber and tracker from Mexico City, had come to Chamonix for a summer of climbing and never left. Jens Melkopf, their team's doctor, had joined them after spending a decade with the German Special Forces. And of course, Kat Barreau was the kind of helicopter pilot who could land the helicopter on a coin, in the middle of a storm.

"It's good to see you too, Rémy. Glad you're both here," Damien said, sobering up. "I think we're going to need your help."

Drake summarized the situation for them. "The missing climbers, a man and a woman, went out early this morning to La Rébuffat. It was the man's first multi-pitch climb, and they haven't returned yet. It's six-thirty p.m. now, which means we have a couple hours of daylight left to find them."

"What are we waiting for, then?" Gael said. Damien understood the younger man's urgency—he felt it, also, although his job was to temper that urgency with caution. The truth was, mountain rescue was intense—the rush was similar to that of leading a hard pitch, except you also knew you were helping somebody in the most terrifying moment of their life.

"I already checked at the Aiguille du Midi station, and nobody matching their description took the cable car down this afternoon," Kat said. "Get in, we'll circle around La Rébuffat to look for them."

Somebody's flash went off in his face. Damien squinted and jumped up into the helicopter, glad to get away from the growing crowd. This was a common occurrence for them, as his team's appearance often caught the attention of visitors. The helicopter's presence, in particular, seemed to feed into people's morbid curiosity as they whispered among themselves, wondering what was going on.

The helicopter rose swiftly into the air. Outside the window, the mountains rose around them, tall and majestic. Damien couldn't imagine living anywhere else—that, along with his mother's illness, were the reasons he'd returned right after university.

Out here, in the mountains, one could walk for miles without bumping into another human being—and yet, never be alone. The dry smell of the rocks, the damp smell of the velvet trees in the summer and the frosty snow in winter, the voices of the people he'd climbed with in these mountains in the past—they were always with him up here.

A few minutes later, Kat spoke over the headsets they were wearing. "Look right, that's La Rébuffat." As well as being an excellent pilot, Kat knew the area like the palm of her hand.

"What is it, a 6a climb?" Damien asked.

Gael and Rémy both nodded. "It's a 6a, yes, but it's a long, technical climb."

"One of our two climbers has apparently never done a multi-pitch climb before," Drake said.

Gael shook his head. "And they chose La Rébuffat for their initiation? That's nine or ten pitches."

Damien said nothing. If they commented further, he'd have to remind his team it wasn't their job to judge people's actions, only to support them in making the right decisions and, where that was no longer possible, do their best to help them if they got in trouble. But nobody said anything else.

"Do we know how they're doing in terms of equipment?" Rémy asked.

"They left most of their things at the refuge. They were spending two more nights there, then going back home."

Kat interrupted them on the headset. "I see something, there, on the south face."

At first, Damien couldn't see anything. Kat's visual acuity had tested at 20/10, so that wasn't surprising. As they got closer, Damien saw it as well—two small, dark shapes huddled on a ledge.

Drake brought out a pair of binoculars. "That's them. A man and a woman. The man is signaling to us."

"They must be three pitches up."

Damien addressed Kat on the headset so everybody could hear. "Can you put the helo down in that clearing below, Kat?"

She nodded. "Of course. What are you going to do?"

"We'll climb up to them and figure out if we can move them. Be ready for take off, we might need to get them to the hospital."

"So who's climbing?" Gael said, rubbing his hands together.

"Is that you volunteering?"

"Always, *jefe*. You know that."

"I volunteer as well, *Commandant*," Rémy said. "We brought a lot of rope with us."

Damien nodded, looking at the two men. They'd both spent the day in the mountains, probably climbing hard, yet here they were, willing to climb again.

Drake didn't say anything. Each member of their team knew his or her strengths. Drake was a powerful athlete, but at two hundred and forty pounds climbing wasn't his forte.

"Gael and I will go up and evaluate the situation," Damien decided. "Drake and Rémy will wait below to help us on the way down."

Kat set the helicopter down smoothly. "Stay safe, guys," she said.

The four men got off, carrying all the equipment they were going to need. Estimating the distance between them and the rescues, Damien coiled the longest length of static line around his upper body.

It'd be cumbersome during the climb but, if there was a chance to bring the couple down that way, they would need a long enough line.

They emptied their packs of anything that might not be essential but left their water bottles, clothing and first aid equipment. They didn't know what they would find when they reached the couple.

Gael, being the strongest climber, led the climb. Damien settled to belay him on the first pitch.

"I free soloed this just a few weeks ago," Gael said, his tone easy, as he started climbing. Damien knew the man was a risk taker, but to hear him speaking so calmly about free soloing, where ropes weren't used at all and any mistake was, by definition, fatal, bothered him.

"Not interested. Keep clipping on to those bolts, Gael," Damien warned.

"Relax, *jefe*. I know what I'm doing, and we're working. I'm not going to take any risks with your life or theirs."

Damien noticed Gael didn't say anything about taking risks with his own life, but chose not to say anything.

Gael reached the top of the first pitch and secured himself to the wall. Damien waited for the thumbs up signal before starting to climb himself. His tight shoulder muscles complained, and he gritted his teeth. If the pain didn't subside, he was going to need to visit a physiotherapist at some point.

He reached Gael and kept climbing—it was his

turn to lead in the second pitch. They'd done this so many times before, they didn't even need to speak. Once Damien had secured himself, Gael began climbing again. Damien couldn't help but admire the ease with which Gael moved, as if he were part of the rock he was ascending. Finally, Gael overtook him, leading in the third and final pitch.

After forty-five minutes of climbing, Damien reached the ledge where they'd seen the couple. He stood up and stretched his arms and legs gratefully. Unlike Gael, who wasn't even breaking a sweat, he felt every one of his thirty-six years.

Gael had already clipped himself to the wall, and Damien wasted no time doing the same. It was over three hundred feet to the ground—a fall from that distance was not something either of them wanted to consider.

The ledge was wider than it'd looked from the helicopter—enough that Damien imagined it'd be a magnificent spot for a picnic. Not that he or Gael were admiring the view right now.

Damien quickly approached Gael and the pair on the ground. He struggled to remember their names— Mr. Reeds and Miss Lefevre.

Gael was speaking calmly to the pair.

"My girlfriend is hurt," the man interrupted, shouting. "My phone doesn't work, we've been here for hours!"

Why do people come all the way out here and expect their phone to work as if they'd stayed in the city?

Swallowing his irritation, Damien kneeled beside the prostrate climber. Her lips were pulled at the corner, but her eyes were calm. He noticed with relief that she was clipped in to a bolt on the wall.

One less thing to worry about.

"We're here to help, Miss Lefevre. Can you tell us what happened?

"Aline," she said, shaking her head.

"Aline," Damien agreed easily.

"We were climbing, doing pretty good time— for us, I mean, we're not competitive climbers. I put my foot on a large foothold and suddenly felt my foot swing out from under me. I heard a distinct pop on the outside of my ankle ... I haven't been able to put any weight on it since then."

Damien and Gael exchanged a quick look. Though both men kept their expressions neutral, they were both relieved.

She might not enjoy the trip down, but we can move her.

Time was of the essence now, however, as it'd be getting dark soon.

The man looked around nervously. "Is it just the two of you?" he asked, looking over the edge as if he expected a flying platform to appear and magically take them home.

"It's just us. Don't worry, Mr. Reeds, we know what we're doing," Damien said confidently. He focused on the woman again.

"Aline, I'm going to lift the leg of your pants and look at your ankle, okay?"

She nodded, clenching her jaw in preparation. As he'd expected, her ankle was swollen and extensively bruised. It was at least a Grade III sprain, but an X-Ray would be required to rule out an ankle fracture.

"Okay, good," he said reassuringly. He dug into his first aid kit. "There isn't much we can do up here to make you more comfortable, but I'm going to put an air splint around your ankle to immobilize it."

Aline didn't make a sound as he slid the splint on over her climbing shoe, but her nostrils flared visibly. She was in a lot of pain.

"Easy now, almost ready." He kept his tone nice and easy. Talking to a rescue was an art—you had to find the right tone to soothe and inspire trust, but not sound patronizing.

While holding her ankle still, he cautiously zipped the splint up, then lowered his head and started blowing air into the inflation tube. He ignored her sharp inhale—he hated causing her pain, but this would make the way down more bearable.

"Can you get us down?" Aline asked, her fingers gripping his arm.

"We're going to get you down," he confirmed.

Behind him, Gael spoke softly to the man, draping a spare jacket around his shoulders. Damien realized he'd been so focused on the woman he hadn't paid enough attention to the man, whose erratic behavior was indeed consistent with a mild case of hypothermia. He must have taken off his jacket and given it to his girlfriend at some point—God only knew how long he'd been sitting out here in just a T-shirt.

Damien nodded to Gael.

"Okay. We're going to hook this rope to your harness, and we're going to belay you down—one at a time. You don't have to do anything—we'll do all the work from here. Just relax and use your arms to push yourself away from the wall if you get too close."

"I can't ... I don't think I can do this." The man's Adam's apple bobbed up and down.

"I know you can do it, Mr. Reeds. And the time to do it is now. It's seven-thirty. Soon it'll be too dark to attempt it, and none of us are equipped to spend the night up here."

As if on cue, the wind picked up. It got cold in the mountains as soon as the sun disappeared.

"Can't you bring a helicopter to pick us up?"

Damien shook his head patiently. "There's no place to land it, and no way to load you onto the helicopter safely. The helicopter is already waiting below to take you to the hospital."

"Trust us, Mr. Reeds," Gael said, looking up from the work he'd been doing preparing the ropes. "We've done this before."

"It'll be okay, honey," the woman said. Despite her pain, it was clear she understood her boyfriend was in a worse place in his head. "You go first."

Her words seemed to move her partner, and he

shook his head immediately. "No. No. You're hurt. You go first. I'll be fine."

We don't have time for this.

"Let's get you settled here, Aline," Gael said, grabbing the coil of static line they'd brought and attaching it to her harness.

"Isn't that rope too thin to be a climbing rope?" the man asked.

"It's static line," Gael explained patiently. "It'll serve our purpose better here."

"Are you ready?"

Damien lifted his radio and spoke with Drake below. "We're going to belay them down, Drake. Be ready for them. Aline's coming down first. She's got a bad sprain on her left foot. We've immobilized it but she can't put any weight on it."

"Understood. Rémy and I will be ready for her."

Working together, Damien and Gael belayed first Aline and then her boyfriend. By the time he and Gael reached the bottom, it was dark, and Damien was wishing he'd worn an additional layer of clothing.

The couple were already settled in the helicopter, wrapped in Mylar blankets. They were holding hands and whispering in each other's ear—Damien thought of what the hut manager had said, and hoped this would become just a story for the couple to tell their children and grandchildren.

Or maybe they'll break up next week.

Either way, it didn't matter. What mattered to him

was that they'd both have the ability to make that choice. That was the single biggest reason he and his team did what they did.

Damien looked down at his watch. His son would probably be getting ready for bed already.

ACKNOWLEDGMENTS

To the reader, whether you've been following the Mont Blanc Rescue stories for a while, or are just discovering them, thank you for taking a chance on this book, and for spreading your love of my books. Your support means a lot to me. If you want to learn more about the series, you can do so here (https://www.jrpace.com/mont-blanc-rescue/)

Thanks, as always, to my beta readers and ARC readers, for always being there for me and sharing their insights and feedback.

To my editor and proofreaders, thank you for helping my story shine. Any and all errors remaining are, of course, my own.

Thanks to Maria Spada for the great cover.